A
Fashionable
Affair

Books by Caroline Linden

WHEN THE MARQUESS WAS MINE
AN EARL LIKE YOU
MY ONCE AND FUTURE DUKE
AT THE CHRISTMAS WEDDING
THE SECRET OF MY SEDUCTION
DRESSED TO KISS
SIX DEGREES OF SCANDAL
A STUDY IN SCANDAL
LOVE IN THE TIME OF SCANDAL
ALL'S FAIR IN LOVE AND SCANDAL
IT TAKES A SCANDAL
LOVE AND OTHER SCANDALS
AT THE DUKE'S WEDDING
THE WAY TO A DUKE'S HEART
BLAME IT ON BATH
ONE NIGHT IN LONDON
I LOVE THE EARL
YOU ONLY LOVE ONCE
FOR YOUR ARMS ONLY
A VIEW TO A KISS
A RAKE'S GUIDE TO SEDUCTION
WHAT A ROGUE DESIRES
WHAT A GENTLEMAN WANTS
WHAT A WOMAN NEEDS

AT THE BILLIONAIRE'S WEDDING

A Fashionable Affair

Caroline
Linden

Originally published in the anthology *Dressed to Kiss*

This is a work of fiction. Any references to historical events, real people, or real locales are used fictitiously. Other names, characters, places and incidents are the product of the author's imagination and any resemblance to actual events, locales, or persons, either living or dead, is entirely coincidental.

ISBN: 0-9971494-3-4
ISBN-13: 978-0-9971494-3-2

Printed in the USA

To my daughter, who will always be more fashionable than
I could ever hope to be

Prologue

Felicity Dawkins had fashion in her blood.

She had been born above her modiste mother's shop, Madame Follette's, and raised among the bolts of silk and lace, picking buttons off the floor and fetching thread for the seamstresses as soon as she could toddle along and name her colors. By the time she was six, she had her own tiny pincushion to tie to her wrist and a small pair of scissors, so she could learn to make little dresses for her dolls from scraps of cloth. By the time she reached ten, she was responsible for mending her own clothing and that of her younger brother Henry, and when she turned thirteen, she began making their clothes as well. At fifteen her mother, Sophie-Louise, made her an apprentice, and taught her not only how to cut and stitch a gown that fit properly, but also how to coordinate colors and embellishments for a harmonious and tasteful finished gown. At eighteen she became a formal seamstress and began taking on clients of her own, learning how to listen to a customer and divine her true wishes, regardless of what she *said* she wanted, and

1

how to steer that client gently but surely toward a style, color, and fit that would flatter her.

And Felicity loved it. The neat little shop in Vine Street was her world, filled with beautiful fabrics and opportunities to create something beautiful each and every day. It was difficult work, to be sure; bending over a dress for hours at a time made her back ache and her eyes burn, as the candles burned low. But it was all worth it when the customer returned and put on the gown for the first time. Felicity lived for the moment her client's eyes would widen in delight as she saw herself in the mirror, and turn from side to side, exclaiming at the line of the skirt and the fit of the bodice.

Unfortunately, at some point those moments started becoming more infrequent. She wasn't sure when; the end of the war, perhaps, when Paris and its styles were accessible again, rendering London's dressmakers a shade less vital. Or perhaps it was the changing shape of women's gowns, away from the light and elegant frocks toward gowns of heavier fabrics with more elaborate decoration. Madame Follette's excelled at the Classical silhouette, crafted of fabrics so fine they were almost sheer. Thick silks didn't drape the same way, and Sophie-Louise clucked her tongue at the puffs and ruching that seemed to sprout like mushrooms on bodices and hemlines.

"No gown needs six rows of ruffles and a tall lace collar," she vehemently declared, tossing aside the magazines filled with fashion plates of beruffled skirts and lace collars that hid the wearer's ears. "It looks ridiculous. I won't have it!"

Felicity might have agreed with her mother on some of these points of fashion, but she did not hold with Sophie-Louise's disregard for the financial impact of this decision.

Women who had patronized Madame Follette's for years stopped placing their usual orders after Sophie-Louise scoffed at the trimmings they wanted. Even worse, younger women, new brides and heiresses making their debuts and country ladies finally able to come to London for a season, did not choose Madame Follette's. To her dismay, Felicity began to see the difference between the gowns from her shop and the gowns from rival shops. While Follette's still excelled all others in the quality of work and fit, now their gowns began to look... plain. Simple. Old-fashioned, even.

This sparked deep alarm in Felicity's breast. Follette's was everything to her, not merely her home and employment but her heart and soul. She tried to persuade her mother to adapt to the changing styles, but Sophie-Louise was having none of it. "Not as long as I am at Follette's," she vowed.

But eventually the facts must be faced: Follette's income had fallen to dangerous levels. Henry, who kept the shop's books, confided to her that they would have to ask for credit from the silk warehouses as well as the lace makers—and there was no good prospect that they would be able to pay it back once they lost their top dressmaker, who finally decamped to another modiste's shop after a fierce argument with Sophie-Louise about embellishing sleeves with puffs for a customer's gown.

Henry didn't say it aloud, but Felicity could read the books almost as well as he could. They were in debt, and their income was declining. If things went on this way much longer, they would be in danger of losing Follette's, and Felicity refused to contemplate that. She told her brother they must convince their mother of the danger she was courting. After her children, Sophie-Louise loved

3

nothing more than her shop, but Felicity prayed they could overcome her stubborn refusal to change.

And to her relief, Henry agreed with her. "I've been worried about this for a little while," he admitted, and agreed to come to dinner that night for the delicate conversation.

"Mama, we are worried about Follette's," Felicity began after the meal. "We have lost five customers this year"—she held up the letters they had sent in response to her queries about orders for the upcoming season—"and gained only one."

"Faugh." Sophie-Louise made a face. "Witless fools chasing after styles that make them look ridiculous."

At this point, Felicity would make any outrageous gown a client wanted, provided it was paid for in ready coin. "That may be, but we need customers. It's well and good for you to frown on the current mode, but that is what people want now."

Sophie-Louise waved her hands irritably. "I won't have my name associated with it. We will get by with our current customers until this madness for fringe passes. Fringe! Puffs! Rubbish. It cannot last more than a year or two, and then everyone will come back."

Felicity and Henry exchanged a glance. "We aren't getting by that well, Mama," said Henry.

Immediately their mother's face softened. In her eyes Henry could do no wrong, which was why Felicity needed him to do this with her. Sophie-Louise would overrule and ignore her daughter's arguments, but she listened to her son.

"Don't worry, Henri," she told him soothingly. "I know what I am doing. Almost thirty years I have been a dressmaker. The styles will change."

4

"And that is why we must change with them," Felicity pointed out. "Please, Mama. I am worried, even if you are not."

Her mother frowned at her. "Worried? Do not be silly, Felicity. I built this shop from nothing—my designs and styles created the reputation of Follette's, and I will not allow it to be transformed into a pale imitation of Madame de Louvier's." She sniffed at the mention of a rival modiste. "*She* is not even French! And no taste or restraint at all. I do not understand how she is still in business."

Felicity understood. Madame de Louvier embraced the style of the moment; whatever her customers wanted, she gave them. Her designs were not inspired or clever, and were often copied straight from the fashion plates of *La Belle Assemblee* without regard for the individual charms of the woman ordering the gown, but she delivered gowns in the latest styles. And for that, customers were leaving Follette's and going to her.

She turned a stern look upon her brother. He didn't like to get in the middle of arguments between the two of them, but this time he had no choice. Henry nodded. "Mama, we are surviving on credit."

"Everyone lives on credit from time to time. We have accounts at all the suppliers for this reason. When the commissions come in, we will be fine."

"No, Mama, we won't." Henry didn't blink as she look at him in surprise. "We have been using credit for a while now. The commissions are not coming in at the rate we need. Mama, we are in danger of losing Follette's." He glanced at his sister. "Felicity is right. We need to change."

Sophie-Louise subsided, her expression troubled for the first time. Felicity tried not to feel annoyed that it took

Henry's word to persuade their mother that she was right. "I don't like it…"

"These are our options," Henry went. "We could sell Follette's—"

"No!"

A faint grin touched his face, and Felicity bit back her own smile. Neither of them wanted to sell Follette's, either. "Very well. We could retrench—move to cheaper premises, cut back on our stock, dismiss Mrs. Cartwright and perhaps Sally."

Privately Felicity wanted this option to be aired and then rejected, for the most part. Mrs. Cartwright had to go, no matter what. She had been at Follette's for many years and was a very competent seamstress, but she had no imagination for design. Sally, the fifteen year old maid of all work, was a harder decision. If they dismissed Sally, Felicity had a sinking feeling she herself would end up sweeping the floors and stoking the fires. They could reduce the fabrics they kept in stock but that would hurt their productivity, as they would have to visit the warehouses more frequently and pay higher prices for each order.

But the one thing they could not do was move to cheaper premises. While Vine Street had grown a little shabby, it was still very near Piccadilly and Jermyn Street, and only a few minutes's walk from Bond Street. If they relocated, it would have to be further away from, not closer to, those fashionable shopping areas, where rents far outstripped what they could afford. Moving would announce to all the world that they were no longer a leading source of fashionable garments, but just an ordinary dressmaker. They would have to lower prices, which would compromise the quality they could offer, and then they really would be ordinary. Felicity would stoke the fires and sew every dress herself before she agreed to this path to ruin.

Sophie-Louise puffed up angrily, as hoped. "Dismiss Mrs. Cartwright! She has been with me since you were a child, Henri! How can you suggest such a thing?"

"Because we do not have the money to keep her," he bluntly replied.

"And Sally sends part of her earnings home to help her family," Sophie-Louise raged on, her accent growing stronger with each word, as it did when she was upset. "How can you be so heartless?"

"They would both lose their positions if we go out of business, Mama." Henry's sharp retort got his mother's attention. She fell back, blinking. Henry was rarely sharp with her, and indeed, his tone was considerably milder when he went on. "There is another option, but it will require some sacrifice from you, Mama... Are you willing to consider it?"

"For Follette's? *Oui*, I would consider anything to save it," declared his mother. "But we will not move premises!"

Henry cast a fleeting glance at Felicity, who nodded once. She all but held her breath as her brother explained. The idea was both their work, but Felicity knew it would be better received coming from Henry.

"You must step down, Mama."

Sophie-Louise's mouth dropped open in shock.

"Not forever, but for a few months—perhaps a year or two. Allow Felicity to run the shop," Henry plowed on. "She wants to bring Follette's back to prominence, but you and she are getting in each other's way."

"It is my shop!" cried Sophie-Louise. "Mine!"

"And it's failing," said Henry gently. "Felicity isn't trying to take it from you, nor am I. But Mama—we've lost so many customers. We are not gaining new ones. We must do something dramatic or we will slowly sink into impossible debt and end up losing the shop altogether."

"But why must *I* go?" his mother wailed. "I am the heart of Follette's!"

"For your own sake." Henry reached forward to take her clenched hand. "Follette's must change, Mama, and I know it will pain you to see it happen. Take a holiday to the seashore. You've spent your life working, you've earned a reprieve."

Sophie-Louise looked at Felicity with reproach. "You want to banish me from my own life's passion."

"No, Mama, not at all. Henry is right: you deserve a holiday."

"A year-long holiday," her mother said sourly.

Felicity ducked her head. "It will take a while to turn things around."

Sophie-Louise looked between the two of them. "You are both against me. How can I win?" She sighed. "Very well, I will go. But I will be keeping an eye on each of you," she added as the siblings exchanged a glance of intense relief.

"Of course, Mama." Henry got to his feet and kissed her cheek. "No one expected otherwise."

Felicity walked him down the stairs, through Follette's. She and her mother shared the rooms above the shop but Henry had taken his own lodgings a few years ago. "Thank you," she told her brother. "I wish she would listen to me and not require your persuasion."

He buttoned his coat and grinned. "Follette's is my concern, too. You shouldn't have to do it all."

"No, I—I want to do it all." She took a deep breath. "I have ideas, Henry. I know I can save Follette's, I know it.

We only need an opportunity to prove ourselves again, refreshed and revitalized, and we'll be one of the top modistes in London."

"We have to make our opportunities," he pointed out. "Time is of the essence."

She sighed. "I know. But we'll find one." *Somehow*, she silently added.

"That's why I supported your plan to take over. I know you can do it; haven't I seen your determination up close every day of my life?" He put on his hat and gave her a grin in farewell. "I've got Mama out of your way, so step to it."

She laughed. Henry opened the door, letting in a blast of cold wind, and strode out into the January night. Felicity closed the door with a shiver and shot the bolt. Her gaze traveled over the dark and silent shop. She *would* save this, she though fiercely. Follette's was hers. Henry kept a keen eye on the books and was proud of Follette's, but he didn't love it the way she did. He had no interest in fashion, and he didn't want to run the shop.

And now that Mama had agreed, Felicity's mind raced. She had to pension off Mrs. Cartwright and hire someone who could bring more flair to their work. She had to scrutinize the latest styles for elements that could be adapted and polished into Follette's own unique signature elements. She needed to refurbish, as economically as possible, the premises to reflect their new direction. And most of all, she needed a significant event that would showcase her work and put Follette's name on the lips of every woman in London. Perhaps the Russian czar would visit again and spawn a frenzy of balls. Perhaps a handful of heiresses would make their debuts.

Ten days later, old King George died. The church bells tolled, the state funeral plans were in all the papers, and

Felicity wrote one word on a piece of paper and pinned it to her wall for inspiration:

Coronation.

Chapter One

Vine Street was a very ordinary lane in London, no longer fashionable and never stately. The brick buildings slumped together in comfortable shabbiness, relics of a frenzy to throw up anything to support the rapidly expanding city. A mixture of shops occupied the ground floors and curtains fluttered at several narrow windows on the upper stories. Vine Street offered cheap lodging and reasonable shopping, a hidden pocket of threadbare gentility only two streets away from the thriving bustle of Piccadilly and the gleaming new boulevard being built from Carlton House toward the elegant neighborhood rising in Regent's Park.

And it was all coming down.

Evan Hewes, Earl of Carmarthen, surveyed it dispassionately as he rode the length of the street. In a year's time Vine Street would look vastly different, with wider pavements and improved drainage, modern sewers, pipes laid for gas, and buildings of clean white stone. There would still be shops with lodgings above, but they would be modern and new, crisply uniform in appearance and no longer a dark hodgepodge of Stuart brick and Tudor half-

11

timbering. It was a new century, and Vine Street would soon be just as new.

The prospect filled him with excitement. Rebuilding always had, ever since his ancestral manor burned to the ground only a month after his father died, and Evan was faced with the monumental task of rebuilding. He soon realized it was more like a shining opportunity. The stone shell remained, but everything within the house, which dated from the time of the Plantagenets, had been wood, and thus burned to ash. Evan moved his weeping mother and younger sister into the dower house and hired a brash young architect who helped him rebuild a house that featured none of the odd corners, strangely shaped rooms, smoky chimneys, or stairs so tight and narrow the footmen couldn't go up them without stooping. Now the manor had clean gracious lines, a modern aesthetic, and every convenience.

He meant to do the same to this grubby little corner of London. It was near the fashionable shops, and once it was rebuilt, the whole area would be revitalized.

The milliner on the corner, the stationers next to it, and the teahouse at the end of the block had all recently accepted his offers to purchase their properties. He already owned almost everything else. There were some tenants who would need to go, but his solicitor had secured settlements with most of them and Evan expected the rest to follow soon. He was giving generous inducements to uproot and move elsewhere.

There was, however, one tenant who had refused all offers. He bent a grim and impatient look upon the premises of Madame Follette's, modiste. It sat near the midpoint of the street, the bow window slightly warped from the settling of the building. The door was painted a bright blue and the steps were neatly swept, but nothing could disguise the careworn feel of the place.

He dismounted in front of the shop. His solicitor had tried for several months to secure the cooperation of the owner, to no avail; when Evan finally declared he would go see her himself, Grantham expressed doubt.

"She's an older lady, a Frenchwoman," the solicitor explained when Evan expressed frustration over the delay. "Stubborn as a mule."

"Offer her more money."

"Tried it twice." Thomas Grantham leaned back in his chair. "In reply she sent a three-page letter that was mostly in French and insulted my intelligence, my manners, and my clerk's penmanship. At the conclusion she refused your generous offer, and for good measure added that she would refuse an offer five times as high."

Evan scowled. If Grantham—who was known for being smooth and persuasive—had failed, the old lady must be a regular shrew. "Did you tell her everyone else in Vine Street has accepted, and the improvements will happen regardless?"

"I did," said Grantham pleasantly. "Her reply to that was a single page of paper containing one word, writ large: *No*. I hope you have an alternate plan, or can demolish and build around her."

By some great feat of restraint he didn't curse out loud. He couldn't demolish around the dressmaker's shop without fatally compromising its structural integrity, as it shared at least one wall with its neighbor. That was part of what made Vine Street so attractive a proposition: Everything needed to come down. He could demolish the buildings on the other side of the street, but the approved plan called for *both* sides of the street to be rebuilt. Leaving one half in place would add insurmountable obstacles, in time, engineering difficulty, and expense, to say nothing of spoiling the elegant uniformity of design he envisioned. The dressmaker had to go.

So here he was, determined to oust the obstinate modiste personally through some combination of charming persuasion and subtle intimidation. He tied up his horse and went in.

A tiny bell tinkled as the door opened, and he stepped into a room that stretched the width of the building. He supposed some would call it bright, and it was for this street, but he couldn't help thinking how much nicer his new buildings would be, when the sun could reach the ground floor windows and illuminate the whole room, instead of only a small area at the front.

But otherwise it was a pleasant room. The floor was impeccably clean, the walls were soft blue, and behind the wide counter shelves held bolts of silk and lace. A selection of periodicals was spread on the counter, and three gorgeously attired fashion dolls stood on shelves near the fabric.

At his entrance a woman emerged from the curtained doorway at the rear. "Good morning, sir," she said, her voice very faintly tinged with French. "How may I help you?"

The answer that came immediately to Evan's mind was rather risqué. If he'd known seamstresses were this attractive, he would have personally escorted his mother and sister to every fitting. The woman before him was lovely, with dark gold hair and vivid blue eyes. He couldn't stop himself from taking a swift but thorough survey, from the top of her blond head to the hem of her skirt. Round hips, trim figure, splendid bosom, and a face he'd very much like to see flushed with passion.

"Sir?"

He snapped his gaze away from her very kissable mouth. *Business, then pleasure,* he told himself. Buy the building, then flirt with the seamstress. "I've come to see Madame Follette."

Her soft pink lips parted in surprise. "Have you an appointment?"

By God, she was beautiful. He leaned against the counter and grinned. "No, but I hope she'll see me all the same." He produced one of his cards and slid it across the polished wooden surface.

A thin puzzled line appeared between her brows as she reached for the card. It vanished as soon as she read it. Her eyes flew back to his, and this time they shone with a more cordial light. "My lord."

"Will Madame see me?" he asked, lowering his voice to a more intimate register.

"But of course!" She smiled, and his stomach took a drop. There was a dimple in her cheek, and he was sure that smile was coy, almost inviting, as if she felt the same attraction he did . . . "I am Madame Follette."

It was so unlike what he had expected Evan was struck speechless. "You?" he said stupidly.

Her eyes flashed, but her smile didn't waver. "Yes. What did you wish to see me about?"

Inside his head Evan cursed his solicitor. An older Frenchwoman, stubborn as a mule, eh? He'd been prepared for that sort of woman. This woman—young and attractive and dangerously appealing—threw him.

But only for a moment. He straightened his shoulders and assumed a contrite expression. "I beg your pardon. I

15

was expecting an older woman. I'd been told Madame Follette was a Frenchwoman about my mother's age."

"Ah." Understanding softened her demeanor. "That will be my mother, who founded Madame Follette's and ran the shop until a year ago. She has taken an extended holiday to the seashore. But I would be happy to assist you. Have you come to inquire about a gown for Lady Carmarthen?"

"Er . . . No." Behind him the bell chimed again.

Madame's face brightened at once. "One moment, my lord," she murmured to him. "Lady Marjoribanks! Come in, Miss Owen has been expecting you. May I offer you a cup of tea?"

"Not this morning," said Lady Marjoribanks as she stooped to set down a ball of gray fur she was carrying. "Midas isn't well today, he didn't want to be alone. I hope you don't mind."

Evan didn't see the slightest flicker in Madame's face as a pair of malevolent yellow eyes winked open amid the gray fur and glared up at her. "Of course I don't mind. Come, I'll show you to a private room and tell Miss Owen you've arrived."

As they crossed the shop, the older woman caught sight of him. "Carmarthen! What are you doing here?"

"Delighting in our chance encounter," he said smoothly, giving her a bow. "A great pleasure to see you again, Lady Marjoribanks."

She seemed amused. "And you, my boy! I hope you've not come to haggle with Miss Dawkins. She's a wonderful girl, so clever with a needle and thread, and if you reduce her to tears, you'll have me to deal with." She shook her finger in admonishment.

"I wouldn't dream of it," Evan replied, covertly noting the way Madame—Miss Dawkins?—flushed and avoided looking his way.

"Very good. Keep an eye on Midas, would you, while I have a word with the ladies about my gown." She turned her attention to the proprietress, still at her side. "I saw the most original style the other day. Four shades of fringe! Do you think Miss Owen could create something similar?"

He couldn't make out Madame's reply as she guided her client through another doorway. With a sigh he rested his elbow on the counter and regarded the cat still crouching on the floor where Lady Marjoribanks had put him. He knew the viscountess was eccentric, but carrying her cat around with her? From the baleful look on his face, Midas didn't seem pleased to be here, and as soon as his mistress had gone he crept under a nearby chair.

Evan tried to use his moment alone to reassess his approach. It galled him that he'd made such a mistake about the owner, no matter what Grantham had said. Still, it could work to his benefit. An older woman might be reluctant to move, but surely a young woman would see the value in what he wished to do. Surely she couldn't like the way her floors slanted, or that her windows only got an hour of direct sunlight every day. Surely a young woman must want modern plumbing and gas lighting. Evan had done his research, and this was one of the oldest parts of Vine Street. There was no record of it having significant improvements in the last several decades, and he certainly didn't see signs of any now that he was here.

On the other hand, he couldn't afford to be distracted by a pretty face and a splendid bosom. Regretfully he pondered that point a moment. There must be someone else he could speak to, if only to persuade them to intercede with the actual owner.

Madame—Miss Dawkins?—emerged. "I apologize, my lord," she said as she went behind the counter again. "Have you come to inquire about a commission? We are quite busy, but I'm sure we could accommodate you." Her hand drifted toward the fashion periodicals.

"No." He paused as another woman burst out of the same doorway where Lady Marjoribanks had disappeared. With a murmured apology she took some of the periodicals and went back where she'd come from.

"That is Miss Owen, one of my head seamstresses," said Madame. "She has a dramatic eye for color and flair, and designs garments unlike anything else in London. Lady Marjoribanks is devoted to her."

"I've come about a financial matter, Madame." He paused. "Or is it Miss Dawkins?"

Slowly her hands curled into fists before she put them below the counter. "Dawkins is our family name. Follette was my mother's name before she married my late father. What sort of financial matter?"

"One I must discuss with the owner. My solicitor has been corresponding with your mother, I believe, whom he understood to be the person holding the deed to this building." He waited a moment, but she just stared at him, her eyes darkening. Too late Evan thought he ought to have heeded Grantham's advice and stayed out of it. He didn't want to make this woman hate him, but he had plans—investors—promises he had to keep. "Where might I find her?"

"Yes, my mother is the owner. But I am managing the shop now." Her chin came up. "You can speak to me, my lord."

"Perhaps I could speak to your man of business," Evan said hopefully. Surely her man of business, or her solicitor, would see reason and help argue his case.

That was the wrong thing to say. Her mouth flattened and she set back her shoulders with a little twitch. "You can speak to *me*," she repeated, a hard stress on the final word.

There was no other choice, it seemed. He nodded and tried to look rueful. "Don't mistake me—it would be my pleasure to speak to you. Are you aware of your mother's correspondence with my solicitor, Mr. Grantham?"

"No."

"That explains it." He gave an abashed grin. "I feared as much, which is what brought me here today. I've a business proposal to make, but your mother is unwilling to listen."

Her expression didn't change. "As I said, I am managing Follette's now; my mother has retired from the trade. What is your proposal?"

He doubted she was empowered to accept it, but she could help persuade her recalcitrant mother. Evan propped his elbow on the counter again and leaned toward her. Lord, she had the most magnificent eyes, and the way her face tipped up to his . . . "I couldn't help but notice your floor slopes and your windows are warped. This building must be nearly two hundred and fifty years old." He knew it was; building records showed it had been built before the Great Fire, one of the small pockets of London that survived unscathed. And from the looks of things, it hadn't changed much since.

"Yes," she allowed, "but it's home. Surely you have a home, my lord, all the more endearing for its quirks and oddities."

19

He didn't mention that he'd had that building completely rebuilt, in part because of its oddities. "Of course! But there are quirks, and then there are . . . failings. The drains in this street are appalling; it must flood in every heavy rain. And there's no gas, I noticed. All the shops in Piccadilly have gas lighting now."

A mixture of discomfort and longing flickered over her face. "That is true. But there are great improvements happening just a few streets away, and I expect the tide will eventually reach Vine Street."

"You are exactly right." He smiled. "Very soon, in fact. That's what I've come to discuss. I have submitted a plan to improve Vine Street just as Mr. Nash is doing in Regent Street."

"Oh!" Her eyes brightened, and a pleased smile curved her lips. "That is very welcome news! And you've come to let the tenants know? How good of you, sir."

"It will be absolutely splendid," he went on, growing enthusiastic as he always did when talking about his plans. "Modern sewers, gas to every building, wider pavements. The shops will be brighter, the rooms above supplied with water closets and pipes for pumps, to say nothing of taller ceilings and perfectly proportioned rooms."

"That sounds delightful," she said in bemusement, "but how will you change the proportions of the rooms?" Her voice trailed off as she spoke.

Evan went for the bold strike. "I would like to buy this building, Miss Dawkins. Everything in Vine Street will be torn down and built anew, exactly as I said—and you're right, it will be delightful, and a vast deal better than this." He swept one hand around the shop.

"What?"

20

He ignored the horror in her exclamation. "Mr. Nash himself approved the plans, and the work will be carried out with his advice. This street is very near Piccadilly, but has frankly grown too shabby to be fashionable. In two years' time, it will rival Bond Street." He paused, but she only gaped at him, her face pale. "I'm prepared to make a very handsome offer, Miss Dawkins."

"No," she said faintly.

"An offer you would never receive from anyone else," he said softly. "This is an old building. The work in Regent Street will disrupt traffic for years and cut you off from the fashionable part of town when it's complete."

"No!" Her expression grew stormy. "You cannot sweep in here and have my shop for the asking! I presume you've come because my mother has refused all your solicitor's previous inquiries"—he said nothing, and she jerked her head in a knowing nod—"and you should know that I agree with my mother. We will not sell Follette's!"

Evan sighed. As pretty as she was in a fury, he didn't have time for this. "That would be foolish."

"Foolish?" She raised one brow in disdain. "How arrogant, to presume you know anything about my shop or my concerns. Good day, sir." She swept around the counter and went to the door. The bell jangled sharply as she jerked it open, and Midas hissed from beneath the chair.

He tugged at his gloves, studying her through narrow eyes. By God, she was throwing him out. "It would be foolish to stay," he said coolly," because I have already bought every other building around you." Her eyes went wide, and he gave a small shrug. "Vine Street is coming down, Miss Dawkins. If you stay, it will come down around your ears, and when the work is complete, yours will be the lone spot of drab in the middle of a gleaming new street,

21

devoid of all the modern trappings I just described. How much will it be worth then? If, however, you accept my offer now, you'll get good—no, *exceptional*—value for it. I could even sweeten the offer by extending you a lease in the new premises at favorable terms," he added.

She swallowed. "When do you expect this destruction to begin?"

"The last tenant will be out by the end of the month." He put on his hat. "I expect to begin tearing it down the next day."

"The end of the month," she gasped. "Why so soon?"

Evan rocked back on his heels. "So soon? I've been acquiring property for almost a year. Did your mother not mention the multiple letters my solicitor has sent her?" She blanched. "No? Because I assure you, this has been several months in the planning." He took out another card and laid it on the counter. "You may inquire with my solicitor, Thomas Grantham, if you don't believe me."

For a long moment she just stared at him, her blue eyes wide and unfocused. "Good day, my lord," she finally said.

Confounded woman. Annoyed, Evan strode past her, only to pause on the pavement beside his waiting horse. "Look around, Miss Dawkins," he warned her, waving one hand at the shop across the street. The tailor had already gone, and the windows of his shop had a blank, dead look about them. "Soon every window on this street will be dark except yours. Soon the street itself will be torn out. Your clients won't be able to drive to your door, and dust from the demolition will seep through the cracks in your windows and ruin every bolt of silk you possess. Do you really want to run your shop under those conditions?"

For answer she closed the door with a snap, and remained behind it glaring at him, arms crossed over her chest. This time Evan didn't even glance at her splendid bosom. "Think about it," he said again. "And when you reach the obvious conclusion, you have my card." Somewhat sardonically, he bowed to her, then got back on his horse and rode away.

Chapter Two

Felicity glared at the hateful man until he vanished into traffic at the end of the street. As satisfying as it had been to slam the door on him, she couldn't so easily shut out his words.

She gave a despairing huff. Her first sight of him was dazzling: tall and handsome, exuding confidence and wealth. Felicity's imagination had run away from her for a moment, imagining all the commissions such a man might have come to make, and she'd got butterflies in her stomach at the prospect of outfitting his mother, his sister, his wife, his daughter, even his horse if that's what he desired. After dealing with Lady Marjoribanks, no request would make her blink.

Instead he'd come to ruin her. Sell Follette's! Move away! The very thing she'd vowed never to do. And all so he could raze it to the ground and build something new, probably with rents she could never afford. Felicity had seen the building going on in Regent Street. While it had cleared away some ramshackle old buildings and improved the general tone of the area, she couldn't help noticing that those pristine new shops had contributed to her own business's decline. Why venture to Vine Street when one could find plenty of shopping only two streets away, situated along a broad, well-lit, perfectly paved boulevard?

And Mama had known, for months, that that—that *predator* was preying on them, but not said a word. Felicity pressed the heels of her hands to her forehead, trying to calm her temper. It seemed her mother had steadfastly refused His Dazzling Lordship, which gave her a vengeful delight, but how could her mother keep such a thing secret from her and from Henry?

Her hands dropped. Had Mama kept it from Henry? "She must have," Felicity whispered. Surely her brother would have told her, even if Mama had tried to swear him to secrecy for some reason . . .

She strode through the shop and into the tiny office at the back. She grabbed a short cloak hanging on a hook and threw it over her shoulders, then tied on her bonnet. She shouldn't leave the shop, but this was an emergency. Stopping only to ask Selina Fontaine, the other head seamstress who had no clients in at the moment, to mind the salon for a while, she headed out to see her brother.

Clutching her cloak with one fist, her lips pressed into an irate line, she strode toward Henry's lodgings. Although they weren't far from Vine Street, the trip required her to cross Regent Street, forcibly driving home the truth of Lord Carmarthen's words. Construction made a mess. The shop would be filthy, even if she swept twice a day. And the familiar buildings that she'd beheld every day of her life would be gone, torn down just because they were old.

She tried not to think of the burst of delight she'd felt for that brief moment when she imagined Lord Carmarthen's vision of new sewers and gas lighting benefiting everyone already living in the street, not merely himself.

25

She knocked firmly on Henry's door, not certain if her brother was awake. He would be soon, she grimly vowed, and knocked again.

"That sounds like my dear sister's way of pounding on the door," said Henry as he opened that door. He was in shirtsleeves and had clearly been lingering over his breakfast. "Good morning, Fee."

Felicity pushed past him. "Henry, did Mama ever tell you someone offered to buy Follette's?"

His eyebrows went up as he shut the door. "No."

She sighed, although she wasn't sure if it was relief or dismay, and pulled off her bonnet. "A gentleman came to the shop today and claimed he's been making Mama offers to buy the shop for months. Obviously she refused him."

"And you thought I wouldn't have told you, if I'd known?"

"No," she murmured, abashed at his frown. "But I had to be sure. If Mama had sworn you to secrecy . . ."

He gave her a deeply disappointed glance, but his frown faded. Henry was extraordinarily good-natured. Sometimes Felicity thought she'd got all the temper in the family, and Henry all the forbearance. "What gentleman wants to buy a dressmaking shop?"

"The Earl of Carmarthen." Felicity held out the expensive card the earl had left on her counter. "Do you know anything about him?"

"No," said her brother slowly, appearing quite thrown. "Felicity, why on earth would an *earl* want Follette's?"

"So he can tear it down. He says he's bought every other building in Vine Street and will demolish them all around our ears. He's got plans for improvements like in Regent Street," she said, trying not to spit out the word "improvements." Those plans would improve things for the landlords and the wealthy shopkeepers looking for shiny new premises. Felicity was dreadfully afraid, though, that those plans were meant to force out her and other ordinary shopkeepers. *Clearing away the rabble*, she thought grimly.

Henry's brow furrowed again. "He's bought every other building? I noticed Mr. White's tailor shop had closed, but never imagined . . . Did you ask the neighbors if that's true?"

She shifted her weight. "No. Not yet. When do I have time to visit the neighbors and ask if anyone's offered to buy them out? Besides, we're one of the few tenants who owns our building." That was thanks to Sophie-Louise's foresight decades ago, when she'd been determined never to be poor or homeless again. Their mother had fled revolutionary France during the days of the Terror, and it had left a deep mark on her mind.

"It would be good to know," Henry pointed out. "If Mama refused him, perhaps others did as well. He may be trying to cozen you."

"Do you think he lied?" Her heart rose hopefully. How she would love to call Lord Carmarthen's bluff, and see his handsome face fall as he realized he'd been bested by a woman . . .

Henry shrugged. "He wouldn't be the first. It should be easy to verify, though. The parish must have records of the deed holders."

"Would you?" She saw his face; he was not enthusiastic about the prospect, but he would do it. She gave him an adoring smile. "You take such good care of us, Henry, and of Follette's. Mama would be proud—"

"Mama," he repeated. "What will we tell Mama, assuming this fellow's claim is true? If he tears down the

27

whole street, it won't be good for Follette's. And to be clear, Fee, I doubt he'd say he owned everything if it weren't substantially true."

Her mood darkened again. "We can't move, not now." The king's coronation was swiftly approaching. No lady of quality planning to attend would want her gown from a modiste in Bloomsbury or Islington. Bloomsbury and Islington, though far more affordable than Piccadilly or Bond Street, smacked of middle class, not the leading edge of fashion. In the last year and a half, Felicity had fought fiercely to push Follette's back to that edge. She had hired Delyth Owen, a new seamstress with a keen, bold eye for design, and promoted Selina, and all three of them had been creating bold new interpretations of the latest styles. They had staunched the decline of their clientele and even attracted a few prominent new clients who placed expensive orders—and absolutely nothing could be allowed to interfere with delivery of those commissions, because Follette's entire future depended on them.

It was not enough for a dressmaker's shop to produce handsome clothing of good quality. To be considered a fashion leader, a modiste must produce exquisite garments of superior quality *for the right ladies*. Outfitting a merchant's family, no matter how wealthy, or a country squire's wife, no matter how beautiful, would not put a modiste's name on everyone's lips. That required patrons of some prestige, although notoriety could be just as good.

From the moment the old king died, Felicity had set her sights on the coronation of the new king. As prince, George IV had proved himself a man of lavish tastes, exceedingly fond of spectacle, and the stories printed in the papers promised that this would be his crowning moment in every sense of the word. With days, even weeks, of dazzling festivities planned in celebration, every peeress and lady of quality would want a new gown or five, gowns they would wear in front of the most rarefied society in all of Britain. Felicity was determined that at least a few of those splendid new gowns would come from Follette's. But to make that happen, she needed to avoid anything that would disrupt work at the shop.

"How much did he offer?" Henry's question broke into her thoughts.

Felicity flushed. "He didn't say. He said he'd give exceptional value and offered to grant us a lease on favorable terms after the reconstruction is complete." She grimaced, absently straightening some of the dishes on Henry's breakfast table. "Which won't be for a year or more."

"Exceptional value," repeated her brother. "I'd like to know what he thinks that is." She shot a furious glare at him. Henry put up his hands defensively. "I didn't say we should accept it. It's just hard to know what the property is worth. And . . . er . . . We might need a mortgage."

"What?" she cried. "You never mentioned that!" Sophie-Louise would be appalled. Debt was evil, in her mind. It was the threat of not being able to pay their accounts that had persuaded her to let them take over the management of Follette's, after all.

"Nigel Martin is tightening our credit," he said, naming the owner of her favorite silk warehouse. "He wants to be paid in full. I wonder now if he knew about this plan for Vine Street and foresaw trouble for us."

Felicity seethed. *Curse Mr. Martin,* she thought, *and curse Lord Carmarthen, too.* She wasn't going to sell her shop. She was going to see those gowns produced, one way or another, even if she had to mortgage the shop thrice over in order to take a single room in the middle of Mayfair . . .

And there her thoughts paused. The middle of Mayfair would not be a step down. If she had a shop there, it would show that Follette's was moving *toward* fashionable London in light of the destruction of Vine Street, not away from it.

Lord Carmarthen wanted her shop very badly. That much was clear from the way he'd come himself and tried to convince her how greatly his plans would benefit everyone in Vine Street. He also knew she wanted to stay, just as he knew she could become a large thorn in his side. For all his bluster about tearing everything down around her, Felicity knew that her shop shared a wall with the building next to it. He couldn't pull down that wall without destroying her property. But it meant he would probably accept almost any remotely reasonable terms she proposed as the cost of moving out of the shop . . .

"I have an idea," she said softly, still thinking hard.

Her brother tensed. "What?"

She gave him a sharp look. Henry was too amiable to send into battle against Lord Carmarthen. Besides, she wanted to best the earl all on her own. It still rankled that he'd asked to speak to her man of business, and only broached his true purpose when she insisted she was in charge of Follette's. "Never mind now. I'll deal with this." She went up on her toes to press a quick kiss on her brother's cheek. "Thank you, Henry."

He still looked wary. "Please promise me I won't have to rescue you from Newgate. Assaulting an earl is a capital crime."

She laughed as she put her bonnet back on. "No, no. It shall be perfectly legal and proper. I've decided the evil earl may help us yet."

Chapter Three

Evan strode into his solicitor's office, still incensed by his encounter the previous day with Miss Dawkins, or Madame Follette, or whatever her real name was. "How much can I tear down in Vine Street without damaging the modiste's shop?" he demanded without preamble.

Thomas Grantham looked up over the top of his spectacles, and put down his pen. "It didn't go well, did it?"

"No." He flung his hat and gloves into the waiting arms of Grantham's clerk. "Do you still have the engineering reports at hand?" Perhaps there was a way to tear down everything except the dressmaker's shop. Evan told himself he had to be coldly logical about this, and not let a stunning pair of blue eyes shake his resolve. Miss Dawkins had had her chance, and she'd refused it. He was convinced she'd change her mind once work began and she was forced to deal with the dirt and noise and upheaval. She would be on his doorstep begging for another chance to accept his offer, which would not be quite as generous the next time.

Grantham looked at his clerk. "Fetch the reports, Watson." The man nodded and left. "How badly?" the solicitor asked, leaning back in his chair and smiling, once the clerk was gone.

Evan glared at him. Thomas Grantham was not just his solicitor but his friend, a fellow student at Cambridge who had tutored Evan to a surprisingly strong showing in mathematics. Grantham had an engineer's mind, precise and logical, but his father, an attorney, had decreed Thomas would follow in his footsteps and read law. At the time Evan had privately thought it sounded dry and dull, but in recent years he'd come to appreciate his friend's training. As his interest in improvements had grown, he'd realized how vital a good solicitor was to the job, and had promptly put the opportunity to Thomas, who accepted on the spot.

This partnership between them put the best of Grantham's skills to full use: He was able to make sense of the engineers' reports and estimates, and he knew how to guide a large renovation through the byzantine bureaucracy of Whitehall. It had been his task to buy all the property and smooth the way for the construction, while Evan dealt with the architects and tradesmen, to say nothing of using his position to get the necessary approvals.

But now Thomas was enjoying Evan's failure to acquire one dressmaker's shop a little too much. "Horribly," he muttered grudgingly, before turning the barb around. "In part because you neglected to tell me whom I'd be facing."

Grantham's brows went up. "Who? The sole owner is Sophie-Louise Dawkins, widow, although she uses her maiden name, Follette, in her business. Is she even more shrewish in person?"

"No." Evan rested his hip against the windowsill and folded his arms. "I never saw *her*, the older Frenchwoman who refused you so belligerently. Instead I made a fool of myself because her daughter is running the shop now, and the mother has left London." He cocked one brow. "That seems like something we ought to have known, don't you think?"

Grantham frowned at the pointed question. "Yes. I sent a man to visit the shop several months ago and he spoke to her. She must have left since then." He leaned forward and rang the bell. "What's the daughter like? I take it she's no more receptive than her mother was."

"Not much, although she forbore to swear at me in French."

At that Grantham grinned. "That must count as progress, Carmarthen. The mother insulted everything but my parentage."

"The daughter threw me out of the shop," he retorted.

His friend laughed. "Now I wish I'd gone! That must have been a sight."

"Even more amusing will be the contortions required to proceed without being able to touch a brick of her shop," said Evan drily. "I hope my memory is failing me, and that that shop does not, in fact, share significant structural support with the building next to it."

The amusement faded from the solicitor's face. Before he could reply, there was a knock at the door and a clerk poked his head in. "Sir—"

"Did we send someone recently to Vine Street to query tenants?" Grantham asked. "Specifically Madame Follette's, the dressmaker shop."

The clerk looked startled. "Er—I'm not certain, sir. But you've a visitor—"

"I'm engaged at the moment," said Grantham, tipping his head toward Evan.

"I believe you'll want to receive the lady, Mr. Grantham," said the clerk.

Evan exchanged a look with the solicitor. A lady? "Who is it?"

"She gave her name as Miss Felicity Dawkins, of Madame Follette's shop." There was a whiff of smugness in the clerk's voice. "Shall I send her in? It will save time, although I could go 'round to her shop if you prefer."

"I should sack you for laziness, Watson," said Grantham. "Instead I'm forced to compliment your timely interruption. Show her in." The clerk grinned for a split second, then closed the door. "Felicity. Such a joyful name for a shrew."

"I never called her a shrew." Evan straightened his posture without moving away from the windowsill. He told himself not to show any sign of interest or pleasure at her appearance. *This is business,* he told himself, and Grantham would catch any betraying sign of weakness on his part. He must keep his mind focused on how obstinately she closed that door in his face, and how she'd glared at him through the window, arms folded under those beautiful breasts . . .

The door opened again and she walked in. If Evan's first glimpse of her had stirred his interest, his second glimpse threatened to knock him senseless. Today she wore a dress of brilliant blue, as rich as the twilight sky over Carmarthen Bay, and the way the skirt swayed as she walked made Evan's mouth go dry. She had already removed her pelisse and bonnet, exposing her fresh complexion—and splendid bosom—to his fascinated gaze. Her dark blond hair was swept up into a cluster of curls that looked soft and tempting, and the smile she gave Thomas Grantham almost made Evan lose his balance.

"Good morning, Mr. Grantham," she said, the hint of French adding a purr to her words as she made a graceful curtsy. "Thank you for seeing me without an appointment."

If Grantham had blinked once, Evan hadn't noticed. "Of course," said the solicitor. He cleared his throat. "Pray, be seated, Miss Dawkins."

With a swirl of skirts she seated herself. "I understand you have been corresponding with my mother, Sophie-Louise Dawkins."

Grantham caught Evan's fulminating look and sat forward in his chair. He would know what Evan was thinking: If Miss Dawkins had come to them, she must have considered her refusal of the previous day. She must have come to accept, or perhaps to bargain.

But the infuriating woman hadn't looked his way once, and Evan could only glare at Grantham impotently and try to signal that the solicitor should bring the sale to a swift and immediate agreement. The sooner this woman was out of Vine Street, the happier he would be.

"Yes, I have, for several months now," said Grantham.

Again she smiled, somewhat ruefully, as if they shared a private joke. "I understand she was not very receptive to your overtures."

One corner of Grantham's mouth tilted. "Unfortunately not." Like a good lawyer, he was letting her speak, waiting to see where she began.

"I must tell you, neither my brother nor I knew anything about it," she went on. "A little over a year ago, Mama decided to step down and turn over the shop to us. She has gone to Brighton and has little to do with Madame Follette's."

"But she does still hold the deed of the property."

A faint flush colored Miss Dawkins's cheek. Evan told himself he was watching her closely to detect signs that she

35

was weakening, and not because he was fascinated by her skin. "She does, but she has also put great trust in my judgment. If I intercede with her on your behalf, I believe she would accept your offer."

"That would be very good of you, ma'am." Grantham paused. "What would inspire you to intercede? Lord Carmarthen came away from his visit to your shop yesterday disappointed."

The flush deepened. Now Evan knew she was avoiding looking his way to spite him. The single pearl earring that hung from her ear trembled. "I did not expect him, and he caught me off guard with his wild declaration that everything in the street was to be destroyed in a few days' time."

Evan shifted his weight and scowled. That was not how it had gone. He hadn't said anything like that.

"However, now that I've had some time to think about it, I believe we may be able to reach an equitable compromise." She smiled again.

"I'm very pleased to hear that." Again Grantham stopped, leaving the next step to her.

Miss Dawkins didn't appear rattled. "It would be a tremendous inconvenience to relocate my shop. Not only is Vine Street ideally situated for my clients and for my employees, but a move would disrupt our work unpardonably. In addition, I have an extensive stock of fabrics and other materials, and it would cost me a great deal to remove it all, to say nothing of the expense of setting up new premises."

"Yes," Grantham allowed, "but that is why Lord Carmarthen made such a generous offer."

"He has offered money," she replied rather dismissively, "which addresses only one of my concerns. The other two

36

are equally important. If, however, they can be addressed to my satisfaction . . ." She raised her chin. "Then I would be prepared to advise my mother, very strongly, to accept your offer for Number Twelve Vine Street so that Lord Carmarthen may proceed with his improvements."

For a moment there was silence. Grantham darted a glance at Evan, who was thinking furiously. Her other concerns were the inconvenience of moving—which he didn't know how to eliminate—and the "ideal situation" of Vine Street—which was by definition confined to that location. "What would be sufficient to your satisfaction?" he asked.

Miss Dawkins hesitated, then turned her head slightly toward him. "To run my business, I require a suitable set of rooms, including space for receiving clients, fittings, a workroom, and storage of supplies. Since I also live above Number Twelve, any new premises must include respectable lodgings. I don't wish to pay higher rent than thirty pounds a year. And, most importantly, it must be located where it will be more convenient, not less, for my clients and employees. Those are the only circumstances under which I shall leave Vine Street."

Grantham looked at Evan, who nodded once. This was what he'd wanted, after all. As hoped, Miss Dawkins had recognized that she had to give way. She even had a fairly reasonable list of requirements for a new situation, which meant she should be able to relocate soon and not delay his plans. He tried not to think about the matter of her lodgings; did she live alone above Number Twelve? She'd mentioned a brother . . . He pushed that rogue thought from his mind.

"I understand, Miss Dawkins, and that is all very commendable," said the solicitor. "But how can you be sure your mother will be persuaded? She was quite firm in her refusal of Lord Carmarthen's last offer."

"She wants what is best for Follette's. If my brother and I assure her this will be to our benefit, she will accept." There was no shade of doubt in her tone. It was still a risk, but Evan thought it was one worth taking. Surely Mrs. Dawkins couldn't prevail against both her children as well as the ravages of construction.

"We can allow some time for you to locate these new premises, Miss Dawkins, but we must know with certainty whether, and when, we will acquire the property," Grantham went on. "His Lordship has contracted with a number of tradesmen who will need instruction. Can you guarantee an answer by the end of this month?"

"I?" Miss Dawkins raised her chin. "I have no time to ramble about London viewing properties, Mr. Grantham. This is a very busy time for us, with the Season in progress and the coronation approaching. I will use my influence with my mother if, or when, *you* locate new shop quarters and lodgings for me."

"I beg your pardon?" Evan lurched forward indignantly.

At last she met his gaze head-on. Lord almighty, her eyes were blue. "You came to my shop personally," she pointed out. "You offered exceptional value for it. You plan to raze the entire street to the ground, and then rip out the street itself. You yourself, my lord, pointed out that Vine Street will be utterly destroyed because you've bought everything else in it and made contracts with tradesmen already. That must have been an enormous investment. After all this, you would be deterred by finding one shop for a dressmaker?"

Evan stared in disbelief. Even Grantham seemed speechless.

38

Miss Dawkins was pleased to have brought them to a stand. "I know you cannot pull down everything if I stay. My shop shares a wall with Number Eleven; there is only a single course of brick dividing one side from the other, and I must tell you, it is not in pristine condition. You may own Number Eleven, but if you try to take it down, you will cause great damage to my property and I assure you my mother would file suit and pursue it forever." She tilted her head at their prolonged silence. "If you want me to leave Vine Street, you should be able and willing to find a place for me to go."

"We're not estate agents," Evan began, his shock at her bold demand wearing off.

In reply Miss Dawkins cast a pointed look toward the door. The bustle of clerks in the outer office was audible. "You have plenty of people to help you find one, sir."

His mouth thinned. She might have grasped that he was going to win the battle eventually, but she meant to make him fight for it. Unfortunately for him, he had no choice but to do it. The indignity and inconvenience would be worth avoiding the ruinous delays he'd suffer otherwise. "Very well," he bit out. "We'll find your new premises."

"Very good. Thank you, Lord Carmarthen." She beamed at him, a sunny but somehow coy expression that did terrible things to Evan's baser instincts. When had Fortune turned against him so cruelly, casting an enchanting siren as the obstacle to his ambitions? If Felicity Dawkins ever turned that smile on him for more seductive purposes, Evan had a bad feeling he would make an absolute fool of himself over her.

With some unease he forced those thoughts away. "Will you require us to find men to move your household as well?"

He'd said it drily, trying to push back against her presumption, but she merely nodded, her blue eyes wide and somber. "That would be very kind of you. Thank you, my lord; Mr. Grantham. You may send word to me when you have located a suitable property for my inspection." She curtsied again and left in a swirl of blue skirts.

The silence was deafening. "Well," said Grantham a full minute later. "I suppose that counts as success."

"Barely." Evan crossed the room and closed the door. "She wants us to do our part before she even begins hers, which may or may not succeed."

"We'll have to make sure of it, then." The solicitor reached for the bell again and rang for his clerk. "Watson," he told the man, who appeared almost instantly, "locate an estate agent immediately. We need to find premises suitable for a dressmaker's shop within the next month."

"Yes, sir. Where?"

Grantham glanced at Evan, who shrugged. "Anywhere." He listed Miss Dawkins's requirements. "And then go query everyone left in Vine Street personally to be certain each and every tenant has made arrangements to be elsewhere by next month. I want to know everything about everyone in the street, to ward off any other unpleasant surprises."

"Yes, sir."

"Tell the estate agent to send his list of properties to let to me," Evan told the clerk. "I'll take care of this myself."

Grantham looked surprised. "I'm sure it's not necessary."

"No." He flexed his hands, remembering the pleased light in Miss Dawkins's face. She did this to spite him, but they had a bargain now. On no account was he going to let her wriggle out of it. "I want that shop closed as soon as

40

possible. If she dallies or delays for months, it will cause enormous headaches—she's right about the structural wall, isn't she?"

Grantham hesitated, then nodded once.

"I'll hold her to her word," Evan vowed. "If I have to show her every available property in London, she'll be out of Vine Street within a fortnight."

Chapter Four

For two days Felicity all but held her breath, waiting to see how the Earl of Carmarthen would react to her demands.

Every time she thought of his stunned expression, a warm bubble of satisfaction welled up in her breast. He was used to getting his own way in everything, she was sure. It galled her to no end that he was going to get his way this time, too. Mama might own Number Twelve, but Felicity had spent enough time around wealthy peers to understand that the world was organized to help them. Eventually he would find a way to pry them out, which meant her chances of getting something in return were at their best right now.

She felt rather proud of herself for coming up with this plan. Instead of being racked by dismay at the impending upheaval, she thought it entirely possible that it would be a godsend. If Lord Carmarthen could find a comparable set of rooms for the low rent she had named, even closer to the heart of fashionable London, Felicity would walk out of Vine Street without a backward glance. It had been her home all her life, but Lord Carmarthen was going to destroy it all sooner or later, and she might as well wring every possible advantage out of the situation.

But that was all supposition and hope. If Lord Carmarthen couldn't locate a suitable alternative, or simply decided it was beneath him to try, she would have little recourse or aid. Henry had checked, and it was absolutely true that Carmarthen had bought, or was in the process of buying, everything else on the street. All the tenants had been given compensation on the explicit understanding they would be gone by the end of the month. Felicity recognized that she had been dealt a losing hand months ago, before she even knew anything was at stake, and now she could only hope her opponent wanted to win graciously.

She was working on a sketch for one of her longtime clients, Lady Euphemia Hammond, when the bell jingled. Loath to stop working—Lady Euphemia was expected later in the day and Felicity wanted to have this sketch ready for her—she cast a hopeful glance at her brother's back. He sat across the office from her, working at the books. As if he could feel the weight of her gaze, his shoulders hunched slightly. He didn't want to go.

That might be her fault. Henry only came to the shop a few days a week to maintain the account books, and today she had taken up the first hour of the day with recounting her visit to Mr. Grantham's offices. By the time she finished relating every detail, her brother looked slightly dazed. Although he gamely expressed hope that her tactic would work, she could tell he thought it wouldn't. He'd been scrutinizing the books ever since, as if trying to find another way out of their dilemma. With a sigh, she put down her pencil, smoothed her skirts, and squeezed past her brother's chair.

The Earl of Carmarthen stood in the shop, his hands clasped behind his back and his head tipped up as he studied the ceiling. Felicity stopped short at the sight. Her irritation with him had obscured her memory of how attractive he was, but as the clear morning sunlight illuminated his face and figure, she was very keenly reminded of it. His dark hair was just long enough to brush the collar of his perfectly cut gray jacket, and when he turned to face her, the light behind him made his shoulders look very broad and strong.

"Miss Dawkins." He bowed.

Squashing the inexplicable butterflies in her stomach, she came to the counter. "Good morning, my lord. How may I help you today?"

One corner of his mouth curled, but his piercing blue gaze didn't falter. "Don't you want it to be the other way around—that I come to help you?"

"Which would help you in turn," she pointed out.

"Indeed." He strolled across the room and rested his hands on the counter. "Are you always so direct in your dealings with others?"

Her heart skipped, and she could feel her face growing warm. "I like to avoid misunderstandings."

"Oh?" He smiled. She'd seen his smile before, but this time she *felt* it, deep inside—which horrified her. "Very good; so do I. Will you come for a drive with me?"

Disconcerted by the warmth of his expression and the unexpected question, she froze. A drive? Why would he ask to take her driving?

"I've located a property that should meet your requirements," he added. "I presume you wish to view it before taking it."

"Oh," she said, then again as his meaning sank in. "Oh! Yes, I would, naturally." What a ninny she'd become for a minute; as if an earl would ask her to go driving for any

44

other reason! Flustered, she turned to fetch her bonnet, and nearly ran right into her brother, coming out of the office. "I'm going out for a bit, Henry. Ask Miss Owen to mind the salon, please. She has no clients expected until later today."

Henry looked past her at the earl. As amiable as Henry was, he was also quite a big fellow and could look intimidating when he wished to. "Where are you going?"

She took a deep breath. "My lord, my brother Henry. Henry, this is Lord Carmarthen, who wishes to purchase the shop. He has found a potential new location for us, and I'm going to inspect it."

Her brother gave her a measured look. He thought she'd lost her mind, leaving the shop in the middle of the day. Either that, or he was in shock that her mad scheme might possibly be working. "Now?"

"As you see, Lord Carmarthen is here and has offered to escort me there."

Henry didn't appear convinced, but he didn't protest further. Felicity shook her head and hurried to get her things. Her fingers fumbled a little with the bonnet ribbons as she tied them. It would have been polite of Lord Carmarthen to send a note, instead of arriving out of the blue and expecting her to drop everything to go off with him. She preferred not to dwell on the fact that she *had* jumped to do so, instead of thinking of her responsibilities at Follette's. She buttoned on her spencer and went back into the main room, where Henry and the earl were standing in the middle of the salon, gazing up at the ceiling.

"I doubt it's unsafe, but it's a sign of decay," the earl was saying. He broke off as she returned. For a moment he gazed at her as if caught by surprise. Felicity tugged on her gloves. She knew she dressed well. Her appearance, she

45

reasoned, was an advertisement for Follette's and as such she took pride in it. Her dress today was simple, but her spencer was a glorious blue and gold damask with a silk ruffle starched into a graceful arch for the collar. She'd made it over from an old polonaise jacket, bought secondhand for the fabric. It must have been a duchess's, and it made Felicity feel bold and confident—something she needed with the earl about.

"I'll keep an eye on it," Henry said. His head was still craned back as he squinted at the ceiling. "Thank you, my lord."

"Of course," murmured Carmarthen, his gaze locked on Felicity. "Shall we go, ma'am?"

He helped her into his curricle in the street. At the corner he turned into Regent Street. The southern end, near Piccadilly, was almost entirely new construction, from the gleaming curved Quadrant north to Oxford Street. Some of the houses were still being finished, and Felicity pressed a handkerchief over her mouth as a cloud of dust rose around them, kicked up by a wagon loaded with bricks. "London's barely fit to live in, with all the building going on," she muttered.

"I daresay this is a better method than having it all burn to the ground," said the earl.

"A fine argument to make to those displaced," she said wryly.

"No? A fire sweeps all away before it, without warning or recompense. Planned improvements, on the other hand, offer everyone an opportunity."

She gave him a jaundiced look. "I have the opportunity to uproot myself and my business. You have the opportunity to build expensive new shops, without having to endure any of the inconvenience yourself."

He laughed. "Anyone who thinks there is no inconvenience associated with rebuilding an entire block of buildings has obviously never done it."

"So this isn't your first time turning people out of their homes?"

The earl's easy smile stayed in place, in spite of her provocative queries. "I've never turned anyone out of his home. However, I have made fair and reasonable offers to purchase in areas that were primed for improvement."

"All at a tidy profit to yourself, of course."

"Of course," he agreed, "but not only to me. Think of the bricklayers and surveyors, Miss Dawkins, the plasterers and ironmongers who were able to pay their rent and feed their families because I employed them."

"How many of them were able to afford the houses you built?"

"Some. But all of them were paid on time, and what they did with their earnings was their choice." He slanted a curious glance at her. "Surely you can't disapprove of providing employment to so many men."

Felicity pressed her lips together. "No," she conceded. "But on that philosophy, we should keep building everywhere, all the time, so that anyone who wants to work may have a job."

"That would be ridiculous. Why build houses or shops where no one wishes to live?"

"Why tear down and rebuild houses and shops that are already occupied?"

He inhaled a deep breath, then let it out, the sound of patience being tried. "Because they are old, Miss Dawkins. Because they are unsound, and often it would cost more to repair them than to tear down and start anew, only this time with modern methods and conveniences included."

"At a tidy profit to yourself," she said again. He was not doing this out of altruism, no matter how worthy he made it sound.

"Surely the man who brings functioning sewers and drains to Vine Street must deserve a little something."

"Perhaps," she admitted, thinking of the gleaming new buildings in the Quadrant, now several streets behind them. "Although so do the people who will be displaced."

"I never said otherwise." He paused. "I couldn't help but notice that your own shop, so dear to your heart, has a leaky roof. Water has been coming down inside the walls and is responsible for the stains on your ceiling."

She darted a wary glance at him. "Yes, but it's been repaired."

"When?"

"Several months ago," she said slowly. It would have been done sooner, except that the leak had been behind a wall hanging in her mother's room, hidden from view. By the time Sophie-Louise left, the damage had reached the ground floor and thoroughly ruined the wall behind several cupboards in the workroom above. Henry had exclaimed over the bills for the repairs.

"I suggest you don't hire those workmen again," said the earl. "It's still leaking. There are fresh signs of damage in your main salon."

Now she regarded him with dismay. "I'll have someone in to look at it."

"Don't you believe me?" he asked with amusement. "Why would I possibly tell you your roof was leaking if it were not?"

"Because it's another mark against the building, a sign that you're correct in wishing to take it down—and for a lower price as well, no doubt." Felicity spoke pertly, but his words gave her real alarm. She knew Number Twelve was old. The floors all sloped, the stairs squeaked horribly, and the back chimney had a terrible draw. If Lord Carmarthen had offered to buy the building next winter, once all the commissions for the Season and the coronation festivities were completed, she would have been far more likely to accept. Now she could only say a prayer that she could stave off structural damage, and the earl's persuasions, for another few months.

Carmarthen grinned. Felicity's gaze lingered on his mouth for a moment before she resolutely looked away. "I give my word not to lower my price," he said. "Though if the leaking roof makes you more inclined to agree promptly, I shan't be disappointed."

She laughed reluctantly. "It does not. There are other reasons why I cannot accept, which I made quite plain to you and Mr. Grantham."

"So you did." He pulled up the horses and set the brake. "I trust you'll keep your side of that bargain as quickly as I've kept mine."

Felicity looked around to get her bearings; she'd been so caught up in their conversation she hadn't paid much attention to where he drove them. It was a small street, quiet and quaint, but now that she thought about it, she didn't remember turning west. "Where are we?"

"Frith Street, near Soho Square." The earl jumped down and held out his hand.

She could only look at him in dismay as her heart sank. "No . . ." Soho Square was not the right part of town. Soho was practically Bloomsbury, even farther from the fashionable customers Felicity desperately needed to attract.

"No?" Astonished annoyance flickered over his face for a moment, quickly masked. "It's an excellent property. The light is good, the rooms are quite large, and the rent is reasonable. And the roof is entirely sound." He waved one hand, indicating a wide storefront of red brick behind him.

Felicity shook her head. "I'm sorry, my lord. It's not acceptable." She ignored the hand he still held out to help her down.

Carmarthen stared at her. "I beg your pardon. It fits every particular you listed—"

"No, it doesn't," she returned quietly. Sitting in his glossy black curricle in the middle of the street made her self-conscious. It seemed passersby were watching everything. "Please take me back to Vine Street, sir."

The earl looked utterly flummoxed. He stepped closer to the carriage and put his hands on his hips. A thin frown creased his brow. "Tell me why you object to this manifestly suitable shop," he said in a low voice.

Against her will she glanced at it again. A gentleman waited on the step, conspicuously facing away from them; no doubt the estate agent with an agreement to let in his pocket. Lord Carmarthen was certainly eager to get her out of Vine Street. And it did look like a handsome shop, with tall mullioned windows that would expertly display wares . . . to the wives of the prosperous merchants who lived nearby.

She turned away. "I'm sorry, my lord," she said, softly but firmly. "It is not acceptable."

"Is that all the explanation you're going to give?" he exclaimed.

"If you drive me home, I will explain." Unlike him, she was trying to keep her voice low. Even though she couldn't possibly bring Follette's to this street, it was a clean and well-kept neighborhood, and she had no wish to offend anyone who lived here.

For a moment she thought the earl would lose his temper. His mouth flattened, his eyes flashed, and Felicity felt her own temper stirring. If he upbraided her in public—

"Very well," he said curtly. "A moment, please." He stalked away and spoke to the lingering gentleman. Then he came back and stepped into the curricle. With a snap of the whip he started the horses. "Explain what was so deficient you could not even set foot in the place."

"The shop itself looked large and pleasant," she said. "Please don't think I found it lacking, particularly the sound roof. The problem is with the location."

"In what way?"

She heard the cynicism in his voice and it poked at her temper again. "You don't understand fashion, if you need to ask."

Carmarthen frowned. "Obviously I do not. What has fashion got to do with shop premises? Is your ability to stitch silk and lace compromised by the general character of the neighborhood? I confess, I'd no idea seamstresses were so susceptible to such vanity, particularly at the paltry rent you wish to pay."

"I don't pay any rent at the moment. Even thirty pounds a year will be an increase."

"Yes," he said—through his teeth from the sound of it—"but you shall have the money from the sale of your current shop."

"Which must also be spent on preparing the new premises, moving my household, replacing any fabric damaged in the move, and many other expenses! And once it is gone, that sum will be gone forever. My mother may well wish to set something aside for her old age; her life's work and savings are invested in Follette's." She glared at him. Only a wealthy man would carelessly brush aside the issue of money.

Felicity's plans, if they came to fruition, would push her family's income back to comfortable levels, but she was keenly aware that the Dawkinses were still far from secure. Until she, her mother, and her brother had healthy sums saved and invested, with a thriving shop to support them without touching the capital, she would not stop tracking every shilling. She couldn't. If they lost Follette's, their options would be too terrible to contemplate.

The earl fell quiet. Felicity felt flushed and irritable, which made her feel awkward as well. She wished they were already back in Vine Street. Carmarthen simply didn't understand. He called her vain—and a mere seamstress—while brushing aside mention of thirty pounds, which was a very handsome bit of coin to every seamstresses Felicity knew.

"What sort of neighborhood did you hope for?"

His voice made her start. She dared a glance at him, but he was serious. He met her gaze, and she sensed he was as disappointed in the morning's outing as she was. For different reasons, no doubt, but somehow it took the edge off her irritation to know that he was honestly trying to satisfy her conditions.

"A dressmaker in Soho Square attracts a very different sort of client than a dressmaker near Bond Street," she explained. "You may wrinkle your brow and declare that it makes no difference in the sort of clothes one can sew, but examine your own habits. Do you patronize a boot maker in Whitechapel? Do you venture to Holborn for your shirts?" He said nothing, but his jaw tightened.

Encouraged, Felicity went on. "I have no objection to clothing the wives of merchants and bankers. Indeed, they are often wonderful clients! But the success of a modiste may fairly be judged by the elegance and status of the ladies she clothes. To have a gown worn to Court is a triumph; to be spoken of in the ballrooms of Mayfair puts your name, and your work, in front of women whose patronage can set the style and ensure a steady stream of other clients."

"So you wish to be near Bond Street."

"Yes," she said, unable to keep the longing from her voice. Bond Street was a bounty of fashionable needs, from milliners and glovers to drapers and dressmakers, but also of bookshops, wine merchants, hairdressers, and jewelers. To be in Bond Street meant a merchant had reached the pinnacle of taste and desirability.

Unfortunately, the rents charged for shop frontage there reflected this fact. The next best thing was to be near Bond Street, and it had been solace to Felicity that Vine Street was only a short distance away, a few minutes' walk down Piccadilly. But now Mr. Nash's Quadrant and Regent Street sliced through the neighborhood, acting like a gleaming wall between the elegance of Mayfair on the west, and the slowly fading area to the east.

Carmarthen didn't speak again until they reached Vine Street. When he stopped the curricle in front of Follette's, he turned to her before getting down. "You never said you wished to be in Bond Street when you came to Mr. Grantham's office."

Felicity's lips parted. Was he trying to blame her for this? "I don't require premises *in* Bond Street," she exclaimed. "I never said that. I was quite clear, however, that I do require a situation that would be *more* convenient for my clients and employees, not less. Soho Square would

53

be a great deal less convenient, as they would all be required to cross the great swath of chaos that is Regent Street. You can see even this short drive has been filthy." She pointedly brushed at some of the dust that had settled on her skirt. "If you were uncertain of what constituted convenience to me, you could have asked at any time."

The door of the shop opened and Henry stepped out. He must have been watching for her return. Felicity beckoned to him, and he jumped forward to help her down from the earl's elegant but high carriage. "Good day, my lord," she said, giving him a curtsy. "Thank you for driving me home." Carmarthen nodded once, but didn't say anything. Feeling unexpectedly let down, she went into the shop.

Henry followed her. "It did not go well, I take it."

Felicity hung up her bonnet and spencer. "He found a shop in Soho Square, and didn't seem to understand why it was all wrong."

Her brother cleared his throat. "Why *was* it all wrong?"

She sighed. This was why she was in charge and Henry was not. She loved her brother, and knew him to be intelligent and thoughtful, but the finer points of the fashion business weren't important to him. Henry was meticulous at keeping the books and he excelled at dealing with vendors and bankers, but he felt as Lord Carmarthen obviously did: A gown was a gown, and where the sewing took place had no impact on the final product. "Because it would mark a decline in the shop's status. Ladies like to aspire to their fashions, and to their modiste. It might suffice to be in Soho Square to start out, before moving up—which means moving west. To move eastward . . ." She gave a helpless shrug. "It would undo everything we've been working to achieve."

"It really makes that great a difference where we're located?"

"Sadly, it does."

"You would understand ladies' behavior better than I," he said after a moment. "His Lordship was disappointed."

Felicity tried not to think that the earl might decide their bargain was too much trouble, and not come back. Perhaps she should brace herself for more demands from the solicitor. "As was I."

Chapter Five

Evan drove home, brooding over the morning's outing. *It is not acceptable,* echoed her voice in his memory. *And why not?* he wanted to argue. Who was she, in decrepit Vine Street, to look down on a perfectly sound shop in Soho Square?

He crossed Regent Street, where traffic slowed to a crawl. He grimaced and waved one hand to clear away a cloud of dust billowing from a block where a new foundation was being dug. Construction had started near Carlton House and was slowly worming northward as Mr. Nash demolished, straightened, and rebuilt the street. And—as Miss Dawkins had said—it was filthy.

Perhaps she had a point. Evan couldn't see his mother venturing through this mess in search of a new dressmaker, not when it was far easier and more comfortable to go to Bond Street. And if his mother, who was a very reasonable woman, wouldn't go, it was a certainty that other, flightier, ladies wouldn't go, either.

On the other hand, Bond Street rents were quite high. As part of the diligence on Vine Street, Grantham had drawn up a list of the rents that properties across London fetched, to see what would be reasonable in the new Vine Street. Bond Street properties had been near the top of the list, which hadn't surprised Evan. He paid the bills his mother and sister accrued while shopping there. If Miss Dawkins wanted to be in Bond Street, she'd need to pay considerably more than thirty pounds per annum.

He turned into the mews and handed off the carriage to a groom. Perhaps he ought to have asked more specific questions about what she wanted before he agreed to this bargain. He thought about that as he went into the house and strode up the stairs to his study. What would he have done differently?

Not much, he concluded. The only real possibility, which he could still elect, was to let Grantham to handle the business. He had already spent far too much time thinking about Felicity Dawkins, often for reasons he didn't want to examine closely, and if he told Grantham to deal directly with her, it would free Evan from any obligation to see her again.

And yet, inexplicably, he didn't do that.

Instead he sent off a note to Mr. Abbott, the estate agent he'd had to leave standing on the step in Soho Square, detailing the sort of property Miss Dawkins wanted. Anticipating the man's first objection, he added that rents up to one hundred pounds per annum were acceptable this time. That could be negotiated with the landlord, once a place was found.

To his relief, the agent was very prompt. The next morning he arrived with a list of properties near Bond Street that might be suitable. Evan told him to arrange viewings, then sent a note to Follette's dress shop informing Miss Dawkins. The best and fastest way to get that woman out of his thoughts was to get her out of Vine Street. Once she was gone, his unwarranted fascination with her would fade. She would be occupied running her shop and he would be occupied with his building project. There would be no more distraction in his life, the way it ought to be.

Felicity received the earl's note as she went down to the salon. The seamstresses often arrived at nine and began work, but she didn't open the salon to clients until later. London ladies didn't shop early. The presence of a liveried footman peering through the window gave her a start, and she rushed across the room to open the door.

"With Lord Carmarthen's compliments," said the fellow as he held out a note.

"Thank you." She fingered the thick paper. Bracing herself, she broke the seal. But instead of the curt dismissal she feared, he wrote that he had located more properties and asked if she would be willing to view them, beginning this afternoon. This time he listed the streets, which were all west of Regent Street, and some were very near Bond Street.

She felt at once heartened and chastened, and resolved to be more diplomatic next time. She must stop thinking of the earl as an opponent and consider him a partner instead. When they viewed these properties, she must be clear and objective about them, and communicate clearly to the earl what was right and what was wrong. *A little explanation goes a long way,* she reminded herself, thinking of how she would approach a client.

"Will there be an answer?" the footman asked. "His Lordship asked me to inquire, and carry back any reply you wished to send."

"Oh! Of course. Tell him that will be perfectly agreeable, please."

The servant bowed and left, and Felicity went back into the shop.

She headed upstairs to the workroom, where her employees were busily sewing the gowns that should—*would*—set Follette's on the path to success and security. Felicity had asked everyone to be here today because it was time to tell them about Lord Carmarthen's plans. His note only made her more certain of what she would say. At her entrance they all looked up.

"Good morning," she said. "I want only a few minutes of your time. I have news."

She caught the worried looks exchanged between Alice and Sally, the two apprentice seamstresses. "Is it very bad news?" Sally asked hesitantly. She had been here for four years, since she was a child of twelve. She'd seen Felicity dismiss Mrs. Cartwright, which had not been a completely cordial parting.

"On the contrary," she said firmly, "I think it's very good news. But first . . . You must all have noticed the changes in Vine Street. Mr. White's tailor shop closing up, for instance."

"And the coffee shop at the end of the street," murmured Selina Fontaine. She had been at Follette's the longest and must be very aware of the recent decline.

Felicity nodded. "All the shops are closing up, I'm afraid." Anxiety seemed to ripple through the room. "The reason for this is a large improvement planned for Vine Street. Someone has bought every other building, and plans to build new sewers and install pipes for gas. To do all this, however, all the buildings must be torn down and rebuilt."

Delyth Owen gasped. Selina's face went perfectly still. Only Alice seemed undaunted. "But ma'am, that'll be a terrible mess. Look at Regent Street!"

"Precisely," Felicity agreed. "The gentleman expects Vine Street to be as fine as Regent Street, and to that end he wishes to buy this building as well." She paused, suddenly uncertain about what she was about to promise her employees, these talented, hardworking women who depended on her. Delyth had left a career designing costumes for the theater to come work for her; Selina had stayed with her through the hardest of times. Alice and Sally were learning a trade, but their wages helped support their families. Not only Felicity's family depended on Madame Follette's, and that meant they were all depending on Felicity's wisdom in making the right decisions.

But . . . She believed Lord Carmarthen to be a gentleman who would keep his word.

"The gentleman who has bought everything has made my mother a handsome offer for this building," she went on, tamping down her doubts. Her first duty was to be honest, but also optimistic. If Delyth and Selina left her before the coronation commissions were completed, Felicity didn't know what she'd do. They had already attracted several excellent clients. Delyth had secured a large commission from the Merrithew family, whose matriarch had been one of the leaders of London fashion in years past, and Selina was working on a number of gowns for the sister-in-law of the Duke of Barrowmore. Those were the sort of clients Follette's desperately needed. "We will only accept it when we have secured a comparable, if not superior, location for the shop. No one's employment is in danger, and neither is any commission your clients have made. We shall be able to complete every gown ordered for the coronation in time. But at some point, Follette's will be relocating from Vine Street."

"Where to?" asked Sally timidly.

"I don't know yet," Felicity confessed. "I hope not far from here. I'm going out later today to view more properties with Lord Carmarthen, who is improving the street. He's agreed to help us locate appropriate premises."

Delyth and Selina exchanged a glance. "You're quite certain everything will work out well?" asked Delyth.

"Yes," she replied immediately. One way or another, she would make it so. "I wanted you to know that we shall not close. No one will lose her place because of this, and indeed, I hope it will lead to even more commissions from society ladies, which will benefit us all. If you have any questions and concerns, please speak to me. I value each and every one of you, and your talents." She looked around, but no one spoke. She mustered a smile. "Then I suppose we should all get back to work."

Chapter Six

Evan turned into Vine Street resolved to remain focused on business today. Yesterday he'd treated it too lightly, so confident had he been that the shop in Soho Square would solve the problem. He hadn't understood Miss Dawkins's position, and he'd made a bad choice. She must have feared as much; during the drive to Soho Square, he'd tried to tease her, and her replies had been a bit tart.

So today he would take careful heed of what she said. They had a bargain, after all, and Evan was keen to fulfill his side of it. He stopped the carriage and went inside the shop.

This time she was waiting for him, stunning in a raspberry walking dress. She said a quiet word to the young lady behind the counter as she tied on her bonnet, and then she turned to him. "I am ready, my lord."

Evan noticed the girl at the counter watching him very closely. He gave Miss Dawkins his arm and led her out to the curricle. "Am I hated by the whole shop now?" he asked, guessing what motivated the young lady's stare.

A faint blush colored her cheeks. "Of course not. Why would you think such a thing?"

"Your assistant is glaring at me." He tipped his hat to the girl, who was watching them through the window. She quickly turned her back, and Evan started the horses.

"I spoke to everyone this morning to let them know what is happening in Vine Street. I'm sure some had begun to wonder; I rarely leave the shop during the day, yet have done so several times this week because of . . ." She paused, clearly searching for the right words to describe it. "You."

He gave a short bark of laughter. "No wonder she stared! You make me sound ominous."

"Oh no!" she exclaimed, laying her hand on his arm. "I didn't mean that."

Her hand seemed to sear his wrist. Evan called himself three kinds of fool for being so aware of this woman. "Excellent," he said lightly. "It would be very distressing to be thought a monster."

She released his arm. "I wouldn't call you monstrous, sir, but disruptive. You cannot deny you've turned things upside down in Vine Street."

He thought about telling her how some of the other tenants and owners had jumped at his offers to buy. They recognized that Vine Street had two futures: It could remain as it was, growing shabbier and more neglected until it became a forgotten little alley overshadowed by Regent Street; or it could be transformed into an extension of Regent Street, just as modern, but shielded from the traffic of the thoroughfare. Sooner or later they must leave Vine Street, and Evan offered them good value to leave sooner.

Again he reminded himself that Felicity Dawkins had a different view, and that arguing his side of the story would only cause more discord. "Only with good intentions," he settled for saying.

"Yes," she said quietly after a moment. "I believe that."

Evan glanced at her from the corner of his eye, uncertain that he'd heard correctly. Her cheeks were still flushed—beautifully, he couldn't keep from noticing—but she was studying him thoughtfully.

"I do," she repeated with some force, as if he'd questioned her. "But I hope you can understand that I— and my mother—are reluctant to move for equally good reasons."

"Convenience," he said. "Security."

"I have four employees. Four women whose livelihoods depend on Follette's, and I am responsible for them as well as for my own family. Your offer to purchase our shop is generous," she allowed, "but my greater concern is to keep the business on sound footing, which requires clients. In Soho Square we would be even farther from Mayfair, making it less convenient for ladies to visit us. Yes, we can sew the gowns anywhere; but to have commissions for those gowns, we must have clients, and my seamstresses must be able to come to the shop in safety. We often work late hours, my lord, and I cannot ask them to walk all the way across London in the dark."

"I see," he said, mildly ashamed that he'd not thought of young seamstresses walking home at night. "I should have inquired more closely into your requirements for a shop, and for that I apologize."

She smiled, the same warm, dimpled smile that had snared his attention the first day he met her. "I accept." Her smile grew, and she gave a rueful little laugh. "When I told my brother about your first visit, he asked what an earl could want with a dress shop. He was right, of course; what could you know about being a modiste? I should have explained my position better at the start."

"I haven't the first idea about being a modiste," Evan admitted. "But I did research property values very thoroughly, and what improvements would yield the most benefit for the longest time."

"That is good sense," she replied. "And good dressmaking sense as well. I don't make gowns that cater solely to the fashion of the moment. A gown can be fashionable while still being timeless, so a woman might wear it for a few years at least, with alterations and different accessories."

"Perhaps we're not so different," he said, pulling up in front of the first shop to let. "We want to make things that will last."

Her lips parted in surprise as he jumped down and held out a hand to help her. "Perhaps not," she said, sounding pleasantly surprised.

Evan grinned. "Let's hope this shop is suitable, then, so we can both carry on."

Felicity Dawkins laughed, and then she took his arm, and Evan felt the strangest sense of something falling into place inside him. What was wrong with him? He was attracted to her—understandably, on purely physical grounds—but even when he tried to suppress it in the interest of furthering his architectural ambitions, talking business with her made him want her more. What lady in London would talk about creating things—even more, openly speak of being in business? Not one he could think of.

She tipped back her head to survey the building, and belatedly Evan did, too. He was pleased to see that Abbott had done better this time, finding a shop that looked every bit as clean and sound as the one in Soho Square, but located just steps from Bond Street.

The door opened and a man stepped out. "Lord Carmarthen?"

"Yes. And Miss Dawkins."

The fellow was already looking at her with far too much interest. "A pleasure, ma'am. Joseph Ferrars, at your service. Won't you come inside?"

"Thank you, Mr. Ferrars." She gave him a bright smile as they went into the shop. As she passed the man, his gaze raked over her in obvious appraisal. Evan tightened his jaw, and made certain to stand between him and Miss Dawkins.

"The salon is large," she said, oblivious to the way Ferrars was staring at her.

"A full fifteen feet from wall to wall," said Ferrars. "May I draw your attention to the windows? Newly glazed, and ideal for display. I believe you are searching for premises suitable for a milliner?"

"A modiste." She leaned forward to inspect the window, and Ferrars stole a glance at her bottom.

"It's a bit dark," said Evan. "North-facing shops always are."

"It has gas lighting." Unperturbed, Ferrars demonstrated the valve on the sconces.

Miss Dawkins walked around the room, studying the shelves behind the counter and the office at the rear. "There are no rooms that could be used for fittings."

Ferrars jumped forward. "Upstairs. Let me show you." He led the way up the stairs.

"Are you the landlord?" she asked him as they walked through three rooms on the first floor. Evan alternated between watching her face for any indication of approval, and keeping an eye on Ferrars.

"As it turns out, I am." Ferrars was watching her, and now he smiled, a rather predatory expression to Evan's mind. "May I ask if you're the owner of the business in question?"

"My mother founded it and now I am in charge." She ran her fingers along a window pane in the large front room. "This is small for a workroom, but it might suffice. The fitting rooms are quite generous."

"Yes, indeed they are." Ferrars glanced at Evan, who was standing with his arms folded. "Are you a partner in the business, my lord?"

"Oh no," exclaimed Miss Dawkins before he could speak. "His Lordship is merely helping me find a new situation. He has nothing to do with the shop. He is . . ." She hesitated, darting a quick glance at Evan. "A friend," she finished.

Evan's private delight at that appellation was instantly squashed by the satisfied look on Ferrars's face.

"And I believe you're interested in taking the lodgings upstairs as well?" the landlord asked as they went back into the corridor. Evan knew this shop was suitable, if small, but somehow he wanted to find fault with it. He didn't like the way Ferrars looked at her, and he didn't like the idea of Ferrars stopping in all the time. The man had keys to the place and he could let himself in at will. Evan told himself he was concerned for the welfare of all the women working at Madame Follette's, but the truth was he didn't want Ferrars prowling about Felicity Dawkins. He could only imagine how hard it would be for a woman, living alone, to fend off advances from her landlord . . .

"Yes, if they are available."

"They are," said Ferrars, "but they're not large. If you are searching for lodgings for a family . . ."

"No," she told him. "Only myself."

"Very good," murmured Ferrars with satisfaction. "Let me show you." He took out a ring of keys and unlocked a door at the rear of the corridor, opposite the stairs to the salon below. "A private staircase, as you see, ma'am." He swept it open and bowed. Miss Dawkins gave Evan a pleased look and started up the stairs. Ferrars turned to watch her go, a focused, hungry expression on his face, and Evan's sour mood condensed into one thought: The problem with the shop was Ferrars. He hoped some other shortcoming would put Miss Dawkins off the place entirely, because he found himself thinking that he'd have to set Ferrars straight, and perhaps post one of his footmen as a guard, if she relocated her shop here.

He brushed past Ferrars to follow Miss Dawkins up the stairs, putting out his arm to block the man when he started to come, too. "Allow us a few minutes to discuss things," he said, in a tone that brooked no argument. With only the tiniest flash of annoyance, Ferrars nodded. Evan pulled the door closed behind him, and jogged up the stairs.

Felicity Dawkins stood in the middle of a modest sitting room. She had taken off her bonnet, and the afternoon sun illuminated her hair into a glowing halo of gold. She turned to face him. "It's a wonderful location."

That was not what he wanted to hear. "Really?" he said vaguely, strolling around the room and taking a look out the windows.

"Oh yes." She came up beside him. "I think it may be suitable."

"You said the workroom was too small. That seems a great failing."

"It's smaller than I would like," she admitted. "But to be this near to Bond Street, I can make allowances."

Evan squinted at something in the street below. "What do you think of Ferrars?"

She paused. "What do you mean?"

He could see their reflection in the glass, his figure dark and hers bright. Her chin didn't come to his shoulder, and she was slimmer to boot. Ferrars was almost Evan's height, and probably outweighed him by a stone. Perhaps her brother would be around enough to keep the lecherous landlord at bay. Perhaps she was accustomed to warding men off and would have no trouble with Ferrars. Perhaps it wasn't his place to say anything at all—and yet . . .

"He seems excessively interested in you," he said abruptly. "I suppose you didn't notice him staring at your—" He coughed. "Staring at you rather boldly."

"No," she said, startled. "Was he really?"

Evan gave a curt nod. "He has keys to every door in the place. I gather your brother has his own lodgings elsewhere, and doesn't come to the shop every day."

"No," she said again. "Henry only comes a few days a week, unless I ask him . . . Are you certain Mr. Ferrars's interest was salacious?"

His jaw tightened, picturing again the expression on Ferrars's face as he watched the sway of her skirts. "If a man looked at my sister that way, I would beat him to a bloody mess."

She said nothing. Evan waited for her to express shock, outrage, disapproval . . . anything.

"My lord," she finally said, "are you actually trying to persuade me this shop is unacceptable?"

"I think I am."

"Because of Mr. Ferrars." She sounded disbelieving.

"Because you are a woman, living alone, with other young women coming into the shop. Perhaps your brother

69

can keep him in line, but it's a risk I would not personally take, if I were in your shoes."

Her reflection turned toward his. Evan darted a glance directly at her. She was gazing up at him with worry. "Do you really think he's that bad?"

A caustic smile touched his mouth. Ferrars hadn't even been discreet about ogling her. "Would you welcome his attentions?"

"No!" she exclaimed with some horror. "Not at all." She cleared her throat. "Well. I don't think this shop will suit me after all."

The tension in his muscles eased as quickly as a bubble popping. Feeling immeasurably lighter and happier, Evan grinned. "Shall we visit the other property?"

The smile that lit her face was real. "Yes."

They went down to the salon, where Ferrars was waiting. "Thank you, sir," said Miss Dawkins politely. "Very handsome, but smaller than I require."

Ferrars's disappointment was obvious. "You'll have trouble finding a larger place this near Bond Street on these terms, ma'am."

"I shall risk it," she told him.

His mouth tightened. "As you wish. Good day to you." He followed them back to the salon, and closed the door with a bang behind them.

"He didn't take that well, did he?" muttered Miss Dawkins.

Evan glanced over his shoulder. Ferrars was watching through the window, and Evan made sure to give him an icy glare. "Never a good sign." Dismissing the landlord, he turned to the woman beside him, who was regarding him with far more warmth than she ever had before. "Shall we walk to the next possibility? It's nearby, and such a fine day."

Her eyes rounded in pleased surprise. "Yes." Evan motioned to a boy lingering hopefully nearby, handing him a coin to watch his carriage and horses, then offered Miss Dawkins his arm and led her toward Bond Street.

"Was he really staring at me?" she asked as they walked.

"Are you calling me a liar?" His eyebrows twitched upward.

She laughed. "Not at all! I only meant that I never caught him."

He glanced at her. "Do you often catch men staring at you?"

"Oh goodness, that sounds so vain." She had a way of wrinkling her nose in wry amusement that Evan found mesmerizing. "It does happen. Many so-called gentlemen have little respect for a woman in trade. More than one has assumed that since I make my own living, I would happily welcome any indecent overtures and propositions."

"Idiots," said Evan in a clipped voice. "I hope your brother sets them straight."

"Sometimes. Henry looks imposing, but he has the kindest heart, and no stomach for beating up a client's husband merely for having wandering eyes."

He scowled. "Your clients' husbands do this?"

"On a few occasions," she admitted quietly, before continuing in a more confident tone. "But my mother experienced it first, and she taught me to defend myself. Never cross a woman armed with pins and scissors."

Evan didn't think pins or scissors would stop a truly determined man, especially not if that man got her alone in a shop he owned. "You shouldn't have to defend yourself against your landlord. Nor anyone, for that matter. If any client's husbands make a nuisance of themselves, tell me."

This time the look she gave him was openly shocked. "That isn't necessary, my lord."

"Carmarthen," he said. "If your brother is hesitant to thrash someone who's harassing you because it might impact your clientele, I'll do it."

"Why?" She seemed to regret the question the moment she asked it; a beautiful blush stained her face, and she put one hand over her mouth. "I mean—"

"You called me a friend, back there," he said when she stopped. "Did you mean it, or was it just for Mr. Ferrars's benefit?"

"Apparently it didn't deter him from staring," she murmured. She wouldn't look at him. "I shouldn't have presumed to call our acquaintance such . . ."

"No." Without thinking he laid his free hand on hers. "It was a pleasant surprise. Can we be friends?"

She raised her head, giving him a wary look. "You want to buy my shop."

"And raze it to the ground," he agreed. "But not without fairly compensating you and seeing you settled into another, equally respectable, shop."

A glimmer of a smile teased her lips. "And you don't mind that I insisted you help with the latter?"

Evan grinned. "It's what I would have done, in your place, so I can hardly hold that against you."

Her eyes widened, her lips parted, and Felicity Dawkins burst into laughter. "Not really!"

"Something like it," he replied, inordinately pleased that he'd made her laugh. "Never waste a strong bargaining position."

"Well!" Still smiling, she shook her head. "I confess, I never thought you'd see it that way."

"I have always respected confidence and honesty. You've dealt fairly with me, and I've tried to do the same with you."

Her smile grew warmer. "I do appreciate that. So often—" She stopped and bit her lip. "Not every man would."

"Am I convicted of being just like every other man?" Evan made a face. "I doubt I have much in common with Mr. Ferrars, for one."

"No," she said at once, still smiling. "I didn't mean to imply that." She glanced up at him. "This has been a very illuminating conversation, sir."

"Carmarthen," he said again, not even sure why he wanted her to call him that. Every time she said "my lord" it felt like a sharp prod to his conscience, reminding him that they were from different worlds. Evan much preferred to dwell on the more pleasant title of "friend," which could possibly lead to something more intimate.

They turned the corner into Bond Street, and Miss Dawkins took a deep breath of pure pleasure. Evan stole a glance at her, and nearly tripped over his own feet. Her face glowed with eager excitement, nothing reserved or hesitant about it.

"I adore Bond Street," she said rapturously.

"Why so?"

She smiled, showing the dimple in her cheek. "Everything that is lovely and elegant and well-made can be found here." She nodded at the shop beside them. "The finest glover in London. And there, two excellent milliners. Jewelers, hatters, boot makers, china and lace and books and drapers!"

73

Evan looked around and saw shops, filled with ladies and gentlemen and servants carting boxes and packages in their wakes. The sight of so much commerce was gratifying, but he also noted the older buildings and how much they could use some improvement. "And that's why you want to be here?"

"Yes. To be in Bond Street signifies that your work is some of the finest in London." She stopped in front of a large window. "Merely strolling down the street is a joy. See how handsome the displays are!"

"Bolts of cloth."

She gasped at his dry statement. "Oh, but look how beautifully they're presented! You can see the glorious colors of this damask, and the print on that cotton. The velvet is arranged to catch the light and show off the rich sheen of the nap."

"Indeed." Evan gave it a closer examination. "Who would have noticed?"

Miss Dawkins laughed. "Only every woman in London. Several times clients have come to me with a length of silk, proclaiming it the most beautiful thing they've ever seen and wanting it made up into something."

"Do you?"

"Whenever possible. It's an extra challenge, of course, but I never like to disappoint a client."

"I feel ever so grateful for my own tailor now," Evan said. "He only asks if I've gained or lost any weight, then sends the finished garments."

Her eyes opened wide. "With no choice of fabric or cut?"

"No. What difference does it make?" Evan lifted one shoulder. "I expect my valet pays more attention to my clothing than I do."

74

"That, I believe," she murmured, studying his coat and waistcoat with a critical eye.

An unwonted thrill went through him. "What fault do you find?" he managed to ask, his mouth going dry as her gaze moved over him. He imagined peeling off each layer of fabric as she watched, perhaps even helped. The idea of her hands sliding over his skin seized his mind like a fever.

She raised her eyes to his. "Color," she said, her voice husky. "You lack color. But your eyes—" She stopped, her breath catching for a moment. "Your eyes are an unusual color, my lord."

Evan barely heard the last two words. She was attracted to him. The flush on her cheeks gave her away; her eyes were wide and dark and her breathing had sped up. Triumph surged through his veins, as potent as the finest whisky. "Thank you," he murmured.

Miss Dawkins—Felicity—wet her lips, and something inside Evan seemed to growl with hunger. If they hadn't been standing, stock-still, in the middle of the busiest street in London, he would have kissed her, and damn the consequences. "Let's go in."

Evan blinked. "In?"

"Inside the . . ." She motioned toward the door, a blush coloring her face. "Inside the draper's shop."

"Yes. Yes, of course." He would have gone anywhere she invited him right then. Evan swept open the door, and led her inside.

Chapter Seven

Felicity took a deep breath as they stepped into Percival & Condell's draper's shop, grateful for the moment to regain her poise. She must have lost her mind, telling the Earl of Carmarthen that his wardrobe lacked anything. Everything he wore was of fine fabric, well cut and expertly made. His outfit today had cost a very handsome sum, even though it was all in dark, somber shades.

And while she thought nothing of teasing her brother over an unfortunate choice of waistcoat, it was a very different thing to stare boldly and wantonly at the earl's figure. She could find no fault there, from his broad shoulders to his trim waist and strong legs. Her mother would smack her if she'd seen how Felicity had studied Carmarthen's trousers—which fit very, very well indeed.

But when she looked at his face, trying to save herself, she only felt more keenly aware of how handsome he was, from the loose locks of dark hair that regularly tempted her to comb her fingers through, to the brilliant blue of his eyes. Felicity had blue eyes herself; she had never thought blue a particularly arresting eye color. But the earl's were different, almost aqua-colored, like the sea on a fine day. And when he asked if they could be friends, and offered to beat up any man who bothered her, Felicity feared she would forget herself entirely and succumb to the spell of his voice and the temptation lurking in his gaze . . .

She took another deep breath. Theirs was a business relationship—a friendly one, but one that would end as soon as their bargain was fulfilled. She needed to remember that while His Lordship escorted her around town, offering his arm and laughing when she was impertinent.

"May I help you?" A clerk approached, his head angled in question.

"We require some color," said the earl. "Or rather, I do."

Felicity flushed crimson. "Fine wool," she said quickly. "Shades of blue and green. Also damask and satins, nothing elaborate or fussy, but elegant."

"Yes, madam." The clerk headed behind his counter and began studying the bolts of fabric on the shelves that lined the walls.

"Elegant," murmured the earl as they followed. "Thank you for adding that. For a moment I had the most dreadful vision of a waistcoat embroidered with chickens or cabbage roses."

She smiled. "I would never suggest that. Everything in fashion must be chosen with the wearer's image in mind: Is he stern? Regal? Fun-loving and a bit rebellious?" The clerk laid three bolts of wool on the counter. "Not this," Felicity told him, dismissing one immediately. "What about that cerulean wool?" The clerk took it from the shelf and added it to her pile. She stripped off one glove and ran her hand over it. "No, the weave is too coarse. Do you have anything else similarly shaded, but finer?"

For the next several minutes she kept the clerk busy, running around the shop finding different fabrics as the bolts piled up in front of her. Carmarthen leaned against the counter and watched in amused silence, his arms folded. Felicity didn't doubt that it was his presence that kept the clerk's attention focused solely on them, even to the point of brushing off other customers begging his assistance. But she'd forgotten how much *fun* it was to shop. At the silk warehouses she had to keep several competing interests in mind: not just the color and the quality of the fabric, but the cost and what she could do with the cloth, and for which client. Today she could think only of the man beside her, and what would suit him.

"What image do you wish to reinforce for me?" asked the earl, when the counter was piled with bolts. "Rebellious, or regal?"

She laughed. "Neither." She had removed both her gloves by now, the better to assess the feel of the cloth. "Something vibrant and bold, befitting a man who would buy an entire street in order to tear it down." She held up a length of royal blue wool in front of his waistcoat. It went well with his charcoal trousers and gray coat. She put it down and studied the selection. "Something elegant and modern, as you wish to rebuild Vine Street in that style." She held up a sage green cloth, woven with a thin gray stripe. She tilted her head, considering it. "I like this one."

"You're very fond of color." His eyes dipped to take in her pelisse, which was as brightly pink as ripe raspberries.

Felicity smiled. "I am. But only those that suit me. When I was a child, my mother made my clothes from scraps." She made a face. "So much white muslin! It was all beautiful, but I got such a scolding when I got dirty."

"Were you raised in the Vine Street shop?" he asked, surprised.

"Yes." She held up a forest green satin with a pattern of leaves in gold thread. "Striking, don't you think?"

78

"Bold and vibrant," he said, echoing her earlier words. "What else suits me?"

Felicity reached for one of the damasks. It was woven in shades of blue, from deep indigo to hints of pale azure. "Rich," she said quietly, holding it up against his chest. "Suitable for a lord."

"I see. But does it match my eyes?"

She made the mistake of looking up. There was nothing regal about the way he was looking at her. Desire, pure and simple, burned in his gaze, and it ignited a reciprocal spark inside her own breast.

No, not ignited. That fuse had been lit some time ago. Felicity had been attracted to men before and been able to squash the spark. But every time she thought she'd got over her attraction to *this* man, it flared back into life the next time she saw him, brighter and hotter. If she didn't keep her distance from it—from him—she'd find herself scorched before long.

She cleared her throat and busied herself with rolling the damask back onto the bolt. "No, not a match. A complement."

"Excellent," murmured the earl. "Send the lot to Cavendish Square, number eighteen," he told the clerk, handing the man one of his cards.

Felicity's eyes widened. "All of it?" she said stupidly.

The earl picked up his hat and offered her his arm again. "You spoke so beautifully of each one, I couldn't choose."

He'd just bought twenty pounds' worth of fabric without batting an eye. The silk damask alone must have cost ten pounds. Forcibly reminded again that they were from different worlds, she took his arm in silence and let him lead her out into the sunshine.

"Here we are." He stopped at the next block of shops and flourished one arm. The same fellow who had been in Soho Square waited in the doorway, although he stepped back without a word as the earl held up one hand.

It was obvious that this shop was superior to the last. It was better maintained, for one, and occupied a corner, with Bond Street traffic on one side and a more sheltered street adjoining it. Unusually, it had large windows facing onto both streets, which meant more light in most of the rooms.

"So many windows," said Felicity in surprise.

"Shall we go inside?" He led her to the steps, introducing the fellow waiting with the keys as Mr. Abbott, letting agent.

The salon was smaller than Ferrars's, but Felicity couldn't take her eyes off the windows. There was even a bow window at the corner, where one could pose a full-sized mannequin in a gown. Already she could envision the displays she would set up to entice passersby to come inside. "A bit small, but very bright," she said, wandering over to inspect the counter. "What sort of shop was it?"

"A millinery shop, ma'am," said Mr. Abbott. "It should require very little work to make it suitable for a modiste."

"So it seems." She turned down the narrow corridor, lined with shelves and drawers, perfect for storing supplies. "There is only one small room. Are there more upstairs suitable for fittings?"

"Indeed." Abbott hurried forward to show them the way upstairs. The workroom was adequate, with plenty of cupboards and two stoves for heat, and three smaller rooms that would serve as offices or fitting rooms. When Mr. Abbot asked if she would like to see the lodgings above, Felicity nodded eagerly. Even though she told herself not to be too easily satisfied, she couldn't see anything wrong with this shop.

The rooms upstairs were small, but included two bedrooms as well as a sitting room. She walked through them, inspecting every inch. When she came back into the sitting room overlooking Bond Street, the earl was alone; Mr. Abbott must have gone back downstairs.

"What do you think?" he asked. He looked very much at home, resting one elbow on the mantel as if posed for a formal portrait—except for the fond smile on his face.

She turned in a slow circle. "I think it might be perfect."

He raised one brow. "Perfect?"

She lifted her hands and let them fall. "It's right on Bond Street. It's smaller than my current premises, but not much. The workroom is ideal, there are three rooms that could be used for fittings instead of two, as I have now, and the lodging is adequate." She smiled in amazement. "I retract everything unkind I ever said about your desire to tear down Vine Street. You are a godsend! Can this really be only thirty pounds a year? I never would have discovered it on my own."

Something flickered over his face. "With the increased prestige and ability to display directly on Bond Street, your revenue will surely increase."

Felicity's beaming smile dimmed. "I hope so, of course," she said slowly. "It's more than thirty pounds, isn't it?"

He flicked one hand. "Not much."

The warmth and goodwill she had been feeling drained away. She just looked at him, speechless with dismay.

He crossed the room to the window. "You'll have a fine view from here. And is this another closet?" He opened a door, revealing a small storage room.

"Carmarthen."

81

Warily he turned.

"How much is the rent?"

For a moment she didn't think he would tell her. Then he raised one hand as if quell any protest. "The owner is asking ninety pounds, but everything is negotiable—"

"Ninety pounds!" Felicity was appalled. No wonder the shop was so perfect; it was far too expensive for her. "Have you any idea how much a seamstress earns in a year? Twenty pounds—twenty-five, if she's talented and hardworking. Apprentices might not make thirteen. Ninety pounds! I didn't want to pay more than thirty!"

"I know," he said in the same soothing voice. "But hear me out: Let me speak to the owner on your behalf. I'll deal with him entirely. This shop earns him nothing by standing empty and he may consider a lower figure."

Felicity felt crushed by disappointment—not only that she wouldn't be able to take this lovely, ideal shop, but because Carmarthen had lied to her. He brought her to this Bond Street shop that was everything she wanted, knowing it cost three times what she could afford. "And when he says no, a shop this lovely is worth ninety pounds?"

He let out his breath, as if holding back his temper. "You don't know that he will."

She did, though. Felicity hadn't the earl's status or wealth to intimidate everyone she dealt with. The shop owner would laugh in her face if she offered a third of his asking rent. "He would have to be a very big fool," she said quietly. "Even bigger than I was, to think this might be affordable." She looked sadly around the cozy, light-filled rooms. "I need to get back to my shop, sir."

The earl didn't move. "Thirty pounds won't get you anywhere near Bond Street. I had to broaden the search."

She headed for the door, and the stairs, and the street. He followed her, not saying anything until they reached the pavement outside. "I appreciate your efforts, my lord," she said there, addressing the middle of his chest rather than meeting his sea-blue eyes. "I wish I could take this shop, but I cannot. I tried to be clear about what I could afford, so as not to waste my time or yours."

He ran one hand through his hair, tousling the dark waves even more. "You're despairing of it too easily."

Suddenly she wanted to be away from him, from his air of wealth and confidence and most of all from the feeling that she had frustrated him yet again. The easy banter and potent attraction that had sizzled between them only half an hour ago seemed a distant memory. Perhaps he hadn't meant to set her up for disappointment, but he'd known all along this shop cost too much and still he'd let her explore and exclaim over each feature and envision herself working and living there. How could he do that to her?

She had to clench her jaw to hide her feelings. She had no reason to feel betrayed or bereft; the Earl of Carmarthen was no more in her reach than this Bond Street shop. "Good day, my lord."

"Where are you going?" he exclaimed as she turned to start for home.

"It's only a short walk to Vine Street from here." A short walk, across an ever-growing gulf between his world and hers.

"Let me drive you," he said.

Felicity shook her head, unable to keep from looking at his offered arm with regret. Part of her wanted desperately to take it and listen to his promises. Another part of her, though, whispered it would only pave the way to greater heartbreak later. "I think I'll walk."

He stared. His arm fell to his side. "As you wish." Stiffly he bowed. "Good day. I apologize for wasting your time today."

It wasn't a waste, she wanted to cry. *It was wonderful—until the end.* She swallowed the words. "Good day."

She walked home feeling as if a dark cloud hovered over her. The elegance of Bond Street gave way to the bustle of Piccadilly, and she crossed the gleaming new Regent Street, at which point she could almost see the cloud close in around her and envelope everything. Two weeks ago she had thought Vine Street a little tired, decidedly old, but also quaint. Now she saw it as it was: paint peeling from doors, clogged drains letting water pool in the street, windows ominously dark and empty compared to the shops in the streets she'd just left. She went into Madame Follette's and was struck by how dim it was after the shop in Bond Street. What a delight it would have been to receive clients in that bright, airy salon . . .

Alice popped out of the corridor leading to the fitting rooms. "Oh, you're back, miss! It's been quiet since you left. Only Lady Giles Woodville came for a fitting."

Lady Giles Woodville was Selina's client, and the sister-in-law of the Duke of Barrowmore—who was Selina's lover. Felicity had seen the way Barrowmore looked at Selina, and thought it was only a matter of time before he married her. Then Selina would leave the shop and there was no certainty Lady Giles would continue patronizing Follette's. Perhaps Selina would patronize her, when she was a duchess . . . assuming Felicity still had any seamstresses to sew the gowns, to say nothing of a shop for them to work in. Delyth had steady work with the Merrithew family, so steady they had requested she move into their Portman Square home for the Season. If she were left with only Alice and Sally to help her . . .

Felicity took a deep breath and looked around her salon. It wasn't big or bright, but she still designed the best gowns in London. Somehow or other, with Lord Carmarthen's help or in spite of him, with or without her seamstresses, she would make it through this, delivering every coronation gown on time and saving Follette's.

She had to. No one else would do it for her.

Evan watched her go and said a dozen curses inside his head. He'd got so caught up in watching her face light up that he hadn't prepared better for the question of the rent, and now it felt like he'd lost all the ground gained earlier in the day. The discovery that she was attracted to him—perhaps as attracted as he was to her—had gone to his head, like a bottle of wine drunk too quickly.

But he'd had to do it. Her requirements were unrealistic.

"Will that be all for today, my lord?" said a voice behind him.

He swung around to see Mr. Abbott standing on the steps. "Yes. I'll inform you if I require anything else."

"Of course." The older man inclined his head slightly in the direction Miss Dawkins had gone. "I thought the lady found these premises highly satisfactory."

Evan's jaw tightened. "She did. It was the rent she found wanting."

"Ah." Mr. Abbott locked the door and put on his hat. "I am familiar with the gentleman who owns this property. I daresay he would be willing to negotiate if you, my lord, would provide a guarantee."

"What sort of guarantee?" Evan frowned.

"The owner is a man retired from the cloth trade himself; I believe this was his tailoring shop for many years, and he still has a fondness for shops dedicated to fashion." Mr. Abbott cast a polite glance after Miss Dawkins. Her raspberry dress stood out in the crowd. "He would likely favor a talented young modiste over other tenants."

"Then why would he want a guarantee?" asked Evan in irritation. Perhaps this fellow was the same as Ferrars, with less than noble intentions toward pretty young modistes.

"He is aware of what a tenuous existence fashion offers. A shop may soar to the heights of desirability one year, then fall from favor the next and leave the owner bankrupted. I have seen it many times," he added at Evan's frown. "The hatters, the glovers, the milliners, the tailors . . . Let one dandy or duchess set fashion on its ear, and people will abandon any tradesman who cannot adjust immediately. A modiste can be ruined by inventory." Mr. Abbott spread his hands. "I don't speak for the owner, of course, but if he were assured a shop would have capital to survive a few years at least . . ."

He could pay the excess rent. It could be called a loan, or an investment, or even extra compensation for her current shop. But he could mark it as an expense of the Vine Street project, where sixty pounds—even one hundred twenty, over two years—was hardly worth noting in the ledger. Evan's mood lifted as he thought about it.

But would Felicity accept? He tried not to think of the most obvious implication, that he would have an enduring excuse to call on her for months to come. He would have to phrase it carefully, just as he would have to apologize for not telling her the true rent before she saw the place in Bond Street.

If Evan had let himself think about it, he would have been unsettled by how important it was to him that Felicity be pleased. He wanted to see that astonished delight on her face again, and he wanted to be the cause of it. Instead he focused on the fact that this would move her out of Vine Street and allow his other plans to proceed. She'd liked it very much, and therefore she should accept any plan that ended with her taking up residence here, for only thirty pounds a year.

"Thank you, Mr. Abbott," he said. "Your advice has been most helpful. Would you be so kind as to let the owner know I expect to take this property, and he should not offer it to others?"

"Of course, my lord." With a pleased expression, Abbott bowed. "Good day."

Chapter Eight

In the uproar over the dressmaker's shop in Vine Street, Evan forgot that he had promised to escort his mother and sister to a theater benefit. When he hesitated, his sister leapt to prevent him from wriggling out of it.

"We never see you," she cried. "One might think old buildings are more important to you than we are."

He had to laugh at that. "More important? Never—but they don't require me to dance with them and their friends."

Emily made a face at him. "There won't be dancing tonight, so you've got to come."

Truthfully he didn't mind. Evan was pleased that they were in London again. With all his projects in town, he hadn't gone back to Wales much in the past year, but his mother and sister preferred to spend the winter there. He *had* been busy lately, and a night at the theater would take his mind off vexing golden-haired seamstresses.

"My goodness," said Emily in awe as they made their way through the crowded theater salon. "Mother, I see the most wonderful gown."

"Oh? On whom?" His mother began rummaging in her reticule for her spectacles. Evan wasn't sure why she didn't just wear them all the time—she was quite short-sighted—

but she reacted with horror whenever he suggested it. Vanity, he supposed fondly. His mother was still a handsome woman.

"The lady in green, near the stairs. I don't know her." Emily stood on tiptoe, trying to see over the crowd. "We should walk past her so Mother can see the gown, Evan."

"As you wish." He offered an arm to each of them and they headed toward the staircase. Lady Carmarthen had her spectacles on, and remarked admiringly on more than one lady's gown as they made their way through the crowd.

"There, Mother," Emily whispered, squeezing his arm in excitement. "Do look—have you ever seen such a striking bodice?"

Lady Carmarthen turned her head, and Evan obligingly angled his body so she could face the owner of the incredible gown without obviously staring—and, to his astonishment, beheld Felicity Dawkins, standing with her brother at the foot of the staircase.

For a moment he did stare. She looked stunning tonight, and not just for the vibrant peacock green silk that clung to every curve of her body. Her dark blond hair was a pile of curls, artlessly arranged on top of her head, exposing her pale neck. Her splendid bosom was on display, with an edge of lace peeking out that sent his mind straight to the thought of undergarments. Her undergarments. Delicate and lacy, yielding to his hands as he kissed her . . .

"Marvelous," said his mother in delight. "We must ask her whom she patronizes. The color is perfect for her, and it takes a talented modiste indeed to cut a gown to flatter so well. There must be someone who can introduce us . . ."

Evan cleared his throat, then had to do it again. Felicity turned to look up at her brother, who was a big tall bloke, and the smile she gave him lit her face with impish good humor and delight. What wouldn't he give to see that smile directed at him, and to have her hand on his arm . . .

"I know who made her gown," he said gruffly. He steered his family away from her, not wanting his mother to notice his reaction to Miss Dawkins. "I'll try to bring her to our box at intermission, if you desire a word with her."

Emily gasped. "Do you know her, Evan? Oh, who is she?"

"Yes, who?" chimed in Lady Carmarthen.

"Let us hurry," he urged, quickening his steps until his sister stopped gaping at him. "We'll miss the opening act if we linger all night on the stairs."

By the time they reached their box, Evan felt a little calmer. It was unsettling that his heart still jumped every time he saw Felicity, and he would really like to stop thinking of her undergarments, let alone kissing her senseless while she wore little else. He was confident Emily wouldn't notice, but if he came face to face with Felicity, without time to prepare himself, his mother would recognize at once that there was something between them—

That thought stopped him short. There was *nothing* between them. They had made peace, but at best theirs was a friendship, not an affair. A little covert lust was nothing, after all; he couldn't act on it without jeopardizing the Vine Street plan, and he was adamant that nothing could do that.

"Who is she?" Emily demanded as soon as the door was closed behind them. "How do you know her, Evan?"

"Yes, dear, who is she?"

He decided it was best to answer directly. "Miss Felicity Dawkins of Madame Follette's dress shop. I met her because her shop is in Vine Street, my latest endeavor."

His mother's eyes rounded. "*She* is the seamstress? Good heavens."

This was the trouble with benefits, Evan thought; one never knew who might attend. "I've no idea if she created the gown herself, but her mother owns the shop and she manages it at present."

"Follette's," murmured Lady Carmarthen. "I didn't know they were still here."

"Do you know them, Mama?" asked Emily in surprise. "Why have we never gone there? I'm sure I'd recall a gown like that one. Oh Evan, can you persuade her to make one for me? I should adore a gown of that color!"

"Certainly not," said her mother tartly. "Not until you're older. And to answer your question, I thought they had gone out of business years ago. Once upon a time, a gown from Madame Follette was the pinnacle of fashion. She had a way with sarcenet and muslin . . . Unparalleled, I tell you. But judging from this . . . Miss Dawkins, did you call her? Miss Dawkins's gown suggests they've refined their look."

"You must bring her to be introduced, Evan!" declared Emily. "Please?"

Evan, who had been digesting his mother's astonishing revelations about the dressmaker's shop, started. "What? Why?"

"How wonderful it would be to discover Follette's before anyone else in town," Lady Carmarthen enthused. "Or rediscover, as the case may be, but they've been out of fashion so long it might as well be a new shop. I must say, the gowns we ordered from Madame de Louvier are perfectly acceptable, but there is something missing . . ." She paused, her brow knit. "Imagination," she said, sounding a little surprised.

"I cannot wait to see if Miss Dawkins's gown is as beautiful from near as it is from afar," said Emily with longing. "Where is she sitting?"

Evan murmured something indistinct to hide the fact that his eyes had been searching the theater for her ever since they entered the box. She ought to be easy to spot—her brother was too big to miss—but he couldn't. Almost frantically his eyes moved over every box within sight. She had to be somewhere . . .

He leaned forward on pretext of adjusting his chair, scanning the theater all the while, and finally picked her from the crowd. There, in one of the lower boxes. Her gown glowed under the lamplight, and her face was bright with interest as she studied the rest of the crowd.

He let out a breath of relief even as he recognized the danger he was in. God help him. She was in trade. His mother wanted to *employ* her. But in trade or not, she was the most beautiful woman he'd ever seen. She made him laugh, she challenged him—and won—and she made him think, as the gas lamps were lowered and the performance began, that if he did nothing and she disappeared from his world, he might spend the rest of his life searching for another glimpse of her.

"Thank you for bringing me, Henry." Felicity gave her brother a smile as they made their way into the theater. She felt a twinge for coercing him into coming with her to this benefit, but only a very small one. Without his escort she would have had to refuse when Lady Marjoribanks offered the use of her box for the evening, and Felicity really wanted to go out.

For days now she'd done little but worry about Follette's future, including too many hours spent pining for the shop in Bond Street and wondering if maybe, somehow, she could afford the rent. Tonight she wanted to think about anything other than shop rents or which of her seamstresses might leave her first or—most importantly—what the Earl of Carmarthen might do next. She had neither seen nor heard from him since the disastrous day on Bond Street. As much as Felicity told herself she should expect nothing else from him, it was unsettling how much she wished he would stop by, just once more, so they could part on better terms.

"I'm sure it's good for you to get out of the shop," said Henry.

"And for you," she replied pertly. Henry must be as worried as she was about Follette's, though in his own way. Besides, Henry looked so handsome tonight, and the Kilchester family would be in attendance.

The Kilchester ladies had patronized Follette's for years due to some service Felicity's grandfather had done the previous Lord Kilchester. Lady Euphemia, the eldest daughter of the family and a true beauty, had commissioned several gowns for herself, and also one for her companion, a young woman named Katherine Grant.

Miss Grant was the sort of client Felicity adored: She had wonderful coloring and a lush figure, and cost was no object to her because Lord Kilchester was paying for the gown. She also had no sense of her physical attractions, judging from the drab and ugly dress she'd worn to her first fitting. Felicity had put her in crimson, cut to display her magnificent bosom, and Miss Grant had looked dazed when she stepped in front of the mirrors.

But when Felicity mentioned the handsome bill she expected to collect from Lord Kilchester for Miss Grant's gown, Henry's face had turned bright pink. Normally when she spoke of the Kilchesters, he merely nodded, as Lord Kilchester was one of the few aristocrats who paid his bills on time. She wasn't surprised to see her brother all but gape at Miss Grant when they met the Kilchester party in the theater's main salon. And it was so rare to see Henry look mesmerized by a woman, as he did now, that Felicity impulsively linked arms with Lady Euphemia and walked away from her brother, to let the full impact of Miss Grant's crimson gown soak into his obstinate male brain.

"Thank you," whispered Lady Euphemia as they walked. "Doesn't Katherine look lovely tonight?"

Felicity smiled. She'd known Lady Euphemia for years. "She does."

"And Hen—Mr. Dawkins looks very handsome in his evening clothes."

"He does," she agreed.

Lady Euphemia sighed happily. "Just as I intended!"

They settled into Lady Marjoribanks's box. Lady Euphemia tended to attract admirers, and she was soon occupied with them, chatting and laughing. Felicity busied herself with examining the crowd, scrutinizing every dress that caught her eye. It was such a shame when modistes took advantage of their patron's desire for the latest style, she thought, feeling a spike of pity for a petite woman in a nearby box. The poor lady was overwhelmed by the decoration on her gown, from the puffed sleeves and lace collar to the rows of ruffles that covered her skirt—all in a strong shade of pink that made her fair coloring fade almost to blandness. Felicity spent a moment picturing a pale blue gown with subtle embellishment, cut to emphasize the lady's graceful arms and neck. Oh, what she could do for that woman . . .

With a blink she moved on. To have a chance to clothe more ladies like that, she had to establish Follette's as the place for personal style instead of an ordinary shop that produced unimaginative copies of fashion plates. Her own gown tonight was part of that effort, cut from a sinfully luxurious bolt of peacock green silk after a customer canceled the gown it was bought for. It had been an extravagance, to be sure, and she'd hidden the bill from Henry to pay it out of her own funds, but already she had noted several women openly admiring it. All she needed was one person to ask where she'd got it.

The lights grew dim and the play began. Since it was impossible to see anyone's gown now, she let herself get lost in the farce, about two young ladies determined to win the hearts of two handsome brothers by any means possible. It was silly but witty, and ended happily, so there was a smile on her face as the lights came up at the interval.

Lady Euphemia went to rejoin her family, escorted by a Lord Waddell, who looked dazed to have her on his arm. Felicity was just beginning to wonder where her brother had gone to when a firm knock sounded on the door of the box.

"Good evening, Miss Dawkins." It was the Earl of Carmarthen. He stepped in, seeming to fill the tiny box. His piercing blue gaze locked on her.

Felicity's heart almost stopped; why was he here and why was he seeking her out? Heart pounding, face flushed, she curtsied. *What is wrong with you?* she chided herself silently. It was a benefit performance, open to all; she should have anticipated the chance of seeing him. As to his reason for seeking her out . . .

She summoned a smile. "What a pleasure to see you, my lord. Are you enjoying the play?"

"Yes. Mrs. Burton is superb."

"She is."

Silence descended. Felicity waited for the earl to explain why he had come, but he only looked at her. It wasn't a bold or rude gaze, but searching, as if he was trying to puzzle out something about her. It made her unaccountably anxious, and with a tiny jolt she realized she wanted him to see her favorably again—as a woman. A woman who spent far too much time thinking about him, and whose breathing became alarmingly erratic whenever he was near. Of course he was attractive—she had known that since the moment he walked into her salon—but even more, she liked him. He was clever and amusing and he listened to her. And in the draper's shop, when she'd held up a bit of blue damask and looked into his eyes . . .

Felicity knew what desire could do to a woman when it caught her in its coils, and as a result she'd spent most of her life avoiding it. Which was not to say she hadn't had flirtations, even an amour; a handsome soldier had won her heart years ago, but their romance only lasted as long as his regiment was in London. A lace merchant had once suggested she marry him, and one of the tailors who used to work for Mr. White, whose tailor shop had been across the street from Follette's, had tried to kiss her several times before Henry put his fist in the man's face. Her mother had taught her to keep men at bay, whether they were lustful husbands or brothers—or in one case, a father—of a client at Follette's.

She had a good idea what a man like Lord Carmarthen would offer her: an affair, perhaps even something formal with a house and a carriage. Follette's clients had included more than one kept woman, and Sophie-Louise had taught her daughter not to judge any woman's choice too harshly. After the last few years of hardship, wondering if she would lose her shop and home, Felicity understood quite well why a woman might take the security and riches offered to her. She had never thought it would suit her, though.

But if Lord Carmarthen asked her to be his mistress . . .

"I have a favor to ask," said the earl abruptly, putting an end to her dangerously tangled thoughts. "Might I present you to my mother and sister?"

Felicity's eyes grew wide with astonishment. "I would be honored, my lord."

He bowed his head and offered his arm, and slowly she put her hand on it. What could he mean by this? She didn't understand it, but as she walked out of the box on his arm, she felt an almost giddy swell of excitement.

"Thank you," he said as they made their way through the crowd. "They have been admiring your gown all evening, and are wild to examine it up close."

She forced a laugh. So that was why he'd come to her. The little bubble of unfounded hopes burst silently in her chest, which she instantly tried to discount. She should be pleased he was willing to present her to his family for any reason, let alone one that would benefit Follette's. "How flattering! It's one of my favorites."

His gaze dipped to her bosom. "And rightly so."

A shiver ran over her skin. Why did he look at her that way if he only wanted her to show his mother her gown? Lady Carmarthen could come to the shop any day and see it in daylight, without missing a moment of the play.

"I also wished to apologize," he said softly as they walked. "I should not have hidden the cost of the Bond Street shop from you."

"No," she murmured. "Thank you."

"I've not given up," he added. "But getting what you want may require some creativity."

She darted a glance at him. "Of what sort?"

"I'm still deciding that," he said vaguely.

When they reached the best circle of boxes, he opened a door and ushered her inside. Two ladies were waiting, and Felicity would have known them anywhere as his family. He had his mother's eyes, and his sister's bright smile was very like his.

"Mother," said the earl, "Emily, may I present Miss Felicity Dawkins. Miss Dawkins, my mother the Countess of Carmarthen and my sister Lady Emily Hewes."

"Thank you for interrupting your evening to come to us," said the countess warmly. "My daughter and I were struck, as if by lightning, by your gown. It is a marvel."

"Thank you, my lady." Felicity curtsied. "It's my own creation."

"So said Evan," cried his sister, giving the earl a fond look. "We begged him to secure an introduction."

Felicity looked at the earl, who was already watching her. Their gazes connected for a moment, his intent, hers uncertain. "That was very kind of him," she murmured.

"Kind to us!" Lady Carmarthen smiled. "I've been less enchanted by my dressmaker every season, and the thought of finding a talented new one fills me with delight."

Felicity tore her eyes away from the earl. What he thought, and what he wanted, would have to puzzle her another time. She fixed her attention on her potential new client. "Indeed. Whom do you patronize now, my lady?"

"Madame de Louvier." The countess brushed one hand down her dress. "She's very skilled at the latest fashions, but I vow, I've never owned a gown that suited me as well as yours suits you."

This, Felicity understood. She recognized the covetous look the other woman cast at her peacock gown. With a keen and unsparing eye, she catalogued the failings of the countess's own gown, and knew she had the perfect opportunity to win Lady Carmarthen's custom.

"Thank you, ma'am. None of my gowns come from fashion plates; every item we create at Madame Follette's is designed solely for the customer who orders it. There is no way a drawing in a magazine can take into account a particular woman's coloring, nor is it designed to flatter her finest features. Follette's believes a gown should do both." She smiled. "Naturally we include the latest fashionable features, but only in creating a gown uniquely suited to the lady who wears it."

"So I see." Lady Carmarthen studied Felicity's gown with admiration. Obligingly, she made a slow revolution on the spot.

"Lovely," sighed Lady Emily. "Mama, may we please visit Madame Follette's?"

"We shall indeed, very soon." Lady Carmarthen bowed her head. "Miss Dawkins, it has been a pleasure. Until we meet again."

"Thank you, my lady. Lady Emily." Felicity curtsied again, and the earl silently offered her his arm. In the corridor, she couldn't resist. "Thank you, sir," she whispered, unable to keep a beaming smile from her face. "It was an honor to meet your mother and sister." It would be an even bigger honor to see them wear her gowns in society.

"One that may soon be repeated," he said with a slight grin. "I daresay they'll visit Vine Street within days."

"How fortunate you've not started demolishing it yet."

He laughed reluctantly. "Am I never to be forgiven for that?"

"Forgiven! Are you admitting it might not be the very best thing that could ever happen to any street in London?" She felt light and happy, which must explain why she was teasing him again.

"I still believe, unequivocally, that it's the best thing to happen to Vine Street in years," he replied. "And I hope some day you will agree with me."

She looked at him from the corner of her eye. His profile was calm and assured, but, as if he could feel her gaze on him, he glanced her way. It was a cautious glance, questioning, curious . . . hopeful.

And suddenly her corset was too tight and her shoes were too big. She missed a step and stumbled against him, and in a flash his arm went around her waist. Felicity inhaled raggedly as he held her close for a moment, and when she raised her flushed face to thank him, every word fled. Carmarthen's expression was taut, his eyes burning bright with hunger.

Felicity knew she should not get involved with the earl, but that gaze incinerated every sane, sensible thought in her mind, leaving nothing but her own desire for him. "Carmarthen," she breathed, unsure if it was a warning or a plea.

He lowered his head until his lips almost brushed her ear. "My name is Evan."

The warmth of his face, so near her skin, nearly made Felicity's heart burst out of her chest. To use his given name was unmistakably intimate. She willfully closed her mind to the more contradictory signs and questions.

They reached Lady Marjoribanks's box and found it empty. Where was Henry? "My brother seems to have abandoned me," she said with a nervous smile.

"I would be delighted to see you home," said Carmarthen, watching her closely.

Felicity imagined her brother sharing a tender interlude with Miss Grant, and gave a nod. "That would be very kind of you, sir."

They went into the box and the earl closed the door. At the rear it was quiet and dim, although the brightly lit stage lay directly before them and the loud hum of conversation during the interval filled the theater. Without a word the earl reached out and untied the rope holding back the drape that could be drawn to provide some privacy. With a soft shush it fell closed, cutting off the light and sound even more.

He turned to her, his eyes glowing. "Do you want me to leave?"

Her heart was beating so hard, her hands were shaking from it. "What will happen if you stay?" she whispered.

Slowly his mouth curved. "Always direct. I admire that about you." He raised one hand and touched her cheek. Felicity's eyes closed and she swallowed hard. His touch felt so good on her skin. "I want to kiss you," he said, his voice a dark murmur.

With effort she pried her eyes open. "At times . . . At times I suspect you don't like me much . . ."

He gave a short, quiet laugh. "On the contrary, Miss Dawkins . . . *Felicity*. I like you far too much for my own peace of mind."

A shiver went through her at the sound of her name in his voice. She let her head tip slightly, nestling against his palm. "And after the kiss?"

His thumb stroked her cheekbone. "What do you mean?"

"Is that all you want?" Her throat was tight, making her voice husky. "A kiss tonight, then tomorrow we return to sparring over the fate of Follette's?"

He moved a step closer. Felicity realized she had unconsciously pressed up against the wall behind her, in the deepest shadow behind the drape. When the earl brushed his fingers over the bend of her waist, she arched her back, all but inviting him to slide his arm around her—which he did without a moment's hesitation.

"My dear," he murmured, drawing her to him. "Don't you realize you've won every match? I've no wish to keep sparring with you about anything. After this kiss . . ." His lips brushed hers, so lightly she gasped. "You tell me what you want to happen."

"And . . . You'll do it?" She looked at him in disbelief.

The earl—Evan—smiled. "Yes," he said simply, and then he kissed her.

His mouth was soft, tempting, seductive. Felicity's lips parted on their own and he tasted her, his tongue making love to hers. Every little worry in her mind about getting involved with him abruptly winked out, like candles doused by a bucket of water. He cupped her cheek in his hand and tilted her head so he could deepen the kiss. Her toes curled inside her slippers. Oh, how he could kiss. She sagged against the wall and clutched at his jacket so she could devote all her energy and attention to kissing him back.

The applause of the crowd made her jump; the second act was beginning. "No one can see us," the earl murmured, his breath hot on her skin as he kissed her throat.

She glanced at the drape. It only partially obscured them, but the lights were dimming, and it grew a little darker in their secluded corner. "What do you plan to do, that no one ought to see?" she whispered.

"This." He pressed his lips to the swell of her bosom above her gown. Quick and nimble, his fingers undid the fastenings holding the bodice closed in back, and then he eased it forward. "Just a taste," he breathed. "My God— you're so beautiful . . ."

Feverishly she stripped off her gloves so she could plow her bare fingers through his hair. Her lungs seized as his tongue traced circles on her skin, closer and closer to the edge of her corset. Shivers racked her body and her nipples grew hard, aching for him to unlace her and put his mouth *everywhere*. "Carmarthen," she said faintly. "Evan . . ."

He curled one hand around the nape of her neck and pulled her near, until her forehead rested against his. "Say my name again," he whispered, his lips almost touching hers.

"Evan," she said on a sigh.

He kiss her, hard and brief. "What now, Felicity?"

She made a soft noise of indecision. She knew what he was asking. Her heart hammered, both at the white-hot pleasure of his hands and mouth on her skin and in nerves at the prospect of taking him home.

"Do you want me to go?" His fingers were massaging little arcs along the back of her neck. "If you do, I swear on my life I'll go and leave you in peace."

"No!" She put her fingers on his lips. "Not that."

His eyes met hers. "I promised I'd see you home."

Desire made her quiver. "Have you changed your mind?"

"Not at all." His gaze dropped for a moment, to her exposed bosom. "I can do one of three things. The first is return to my mother and sister and allow you to watch the remainder of the performance, before summoning a hackney coach to deliver you home in dignified safety."

She wouldn't be able to pay attention to a word of the play now, not with the memory of his touch still scalding her skin. She gave a tiny shake of her head.

A grin, more feral than amused, flashed across his face. "The second choice is that I escort you home now, as I promised, and then return to my mother and sister."

That one was also not appealing. A few frantic kisses in the carriage wouldn't satisfy her now. "And third?" she asked, her voice husky and hesitant.

He inhaled slowly. "Third . . . I will go make arrangements now for a suitable escort home for my mother and sister, and then I shall take you back to Vine Street and make love to you for the rest of the night."

"Yes," she whispered, almost before he finished speaking. "The third."

With a muffled growl, he kissed her once more, so deeply and so well she wobbled on her feet when he released her. With a devilish smile playing over his lips, he turned her to face the wall and gently tugged her gown back into place. "I'll only be gone a few minutes," he breathed, kissing the nape of her neck as he did up the hooks and ties again. "Wait for me here."

Felicity barely managed to nod before he left, opening and closing the door with a soft click behind him. She rested her cheek against the gaudy wallpaper, dazed and half disbelieving what had just happened. The Earl of

Carmarthen—Evan—wanted her. He was going to take her home and make love to her. The mere thought made her heart pound; giddy anticipation coiled in her belly, and she felt the most insane urge to burst out laughing in sheer joy.

She pushed away from the wall and smoothed her hair, albeit with trembling hands. Thank goodness Henry wasn't here. She was so flustered over the prospect of having Evan in her bed, she couldn't even wonder where her brother had gone or what he was doing. Hopefully it was something so diverting he wouldn't pester her tomorrow about what had happened with the earl.

And if Henry was off making love to Miss Grant, there wasn't a word Felicity would say to tease him about it.

Chapter Nine

By the time Evan returned, she had composed herself enough to leave the theater with dignity. Neither said a word as they went down the stairs, now almost deserted during the performance, pausing at the cloakroom to retrieve her cloak, and then proceeding out to the street, where the Carmarthen carriage awaited. He must have sent for it when he left Lady Marjoribanks's box. Silently he handed her inside, then climbed in and sat beside her.

"What did you tell your mother?" she asked softly, as the carriage rocked forward. It occurred to Felicity that if Lady Carmarthen knew she was the earl's lover, it might end any chance of the countess patronizing Follette's. She still wanted him too badly to change her course, but her practical side regretted that consequence.

It was too dark to see his face clearly. "I told her something unforeseen had arisen and I needed to address it at once."

Unforeseen. She smiled wryly at that. "I see."

"Do you?" His teeth flashed white in the dim carriage as he grinned. "I also made a silent promise that I would remove your gown very carefully, to avoid tearing it. My mother can forgive a fit of passion, but not the ruin of a splendid gown."

"I like your mother very much," she said with a short, surprised laugh.

He laughed, too, then sobered. "Felicity. You said something earlier about after the kiss—that tomorrow we would return to sparring over the fate of Madame Follette's. I don't want that to happen."

Felicity went very still. "Nor do I."

He turned on the seat to face her, and reached for her hand. "I can't stop the plans to tear down and rebuild Vine Street; there are other investors, and the Crown has approved the plan. But I made you a promise, and I will keep it."

"Creatively," she said after a moment, remembering his earlier words.

One corner of his mouth curled upward. "Yes."

She hesitated, but when he looked at her like this, he undercut all her righteous indignation. "Very well. I shall be patient and trust you."

"Thank God," he murmured, reaching for her. "I do mean to satisfy you . . ."

She wound her arms around his neck as he shifted his weight, dragging her on top of him until they sprawled across the carriage seat. "You can start tonight."

"I intend to," he said, and then his mouth was on hers, seductive and lazy, as if he meant to take all night to savor her. Felicity shivered as the thought sent molten heat coursing through her.

It was only a short drive from the theater to Vine Street. Still, Felicity felt as if a year instead of a few hours had passed since she left with Henry. Evan spoke to his coachman as she fumbled in her cloak pocket for her latchkey, and then he stepped up behind her, raising one of the carriage lanterns so she could see. Gratefully she unlocked the door and let them in. With a clatter of hooves and wheels, the carriage drove off as the earl closed the door behind them.

"Your brother lives elsewhere, I believe?" he said.

"Yes." Felicity watched, off balance and somewhat dazed, as he slid the bolt of the lock home.

A small smile played around his lips. "Show me your shop."

Her eyes rounded. "Now?"

"Why not?" He prowled toward her. "I'm curious."

"Well." Flustered, she waved one arm. "This is the salon." He chuckled. "There is the office," she went on, pointing it out, "and here are fitting rooms and our fabric closet." He followed her as she walked down the narrow corridor past those rooms. "Upstairs is the workroom," she said, going up the stairs. Did he really care to see all this? Henry's incredulous query—*what would an earl want with a dress shop?*—echoed in her mind. "And my lodgings are above."

"Show me," he said softly, remaining on the landing when she started to continue up the stairs to her personal quarters.

"Why?" she blurted out.

"Because it's where you spend your days. I want to understand what's important to you."

Felicity hesitated. In the lantern light, his face was focused on her, his eyes darker than usual. She took one step down, then another. "Very well."

The workroom occupied almost the entire floor. She led the way past the cupboards full of sewing supplies and the long worktable, to the wide windows overlooking the street. "Here is where most of the work is done." She gestured at the chairs set near the window. "Alice and Sally, my apprentices, do much of the basic sewing, although Mrs. Fontaine, Miss Owen, and I do a great deal as well."

"Do you still sew?"

"Of course," she said with surprise. "The only way to craft a beautiful gown is piece by piece. If one doesn't know precisely how to cut and drape and stitch the cloth, it will never resemble the sketch. I presume you must know something about how a house is built, in order to plan ones with sufficient space for all your modern plumbing and such."

His grin was white in the darkness. "Of course. But I don't do the plumbing."

She laughed. "A gown is far simpler than a house, I suppose."

It wasn't too dark for her to see the way his gaze slid over her. "Simpler, perhaps, but no less demanding."

Her skin prickled when he looked at her that way.

"They don't sew at the table?" He held up the lantern, illuminating the long, narrow worktable.

"No, that is for cutting. A good table is essential for cutting properly."

He skimmed one hand across it. "And what is this?" He swung the lamp toward an alcove opposite the fireplace. The room glowed as the light was reflected in the triptych of tall mirrors that stood there.

"It's a sort of fitting area." She crossed the room. "For an intricate gown, a client would stand upon this stool in her undress." She stepped up on it in illustration. "We make an initial pattern for the gown out of muslin by draping and pinning it to her figure, marking on the fabric where trim and embellishments should be. With the mirrors, a seamstress can see every side of the gown at once, as can the client. This way there are no

109

misunderstandings about where the trims will be or how low the bodice is."

"Ah." He set the lantern on the small table nearby, meant to hold pins and other supplies. His arms came around her and tugged loose the bow holding her cloak closed. The cloak slid from her shoulders, and he tossed it behind him onto the worktable. "So if you were my client, you would come in and remove your gown."

Felicity's heart seemed to pause, then slam into her breastbone as she felt his hands at the back of her gown, untying and unhooking again. Unlike in the theater, where there had been a fevered haste to his actions, this time he was unhurried and deliberate. *I want to make love to you for the rest of the night.* "Yes."

His gleaming gaze connected with hers in the mirror. "Show me."

Trying to hide the faint tremor of her fingers, Felicity eased the delicate sleeves down her arms, the silk whispering over her skin and leaving a trail of gooseflesh in its wake. The earl—Evan—inhaled sharply as she eased it over her hips, letting it fall down over her petticoats. She almost lost her balance on the step stool as she stepped out of it, but his hands were at her waist, steadying her.

"For an evening gown," she said, "we would work over a lady's undress."

"Hm." His hands spanned her waist, then drifted up the front of her ribs. Standing on the stool, Felicity was the same height as he was. "This tormented me tonight." He ran one finger across the twist of fine net trim edging the bodice of her petticoat. "It winked at me like a beacon until I could scarcely look away."

She was having trouble breathing. "That was not my intent . . ."

110

"No?" His smile was wicked, his eyes heavy-lidded but intense. He bent his head and nipped the sensitive skin at the curve of her neck, and Felicity gave a gasping moan of pleasure. "That's what it made me feel," Evan whispered, his lips brushing the spot. "This is what it made me want."

Her breath shuddered as she watched in the mirror, his hands dark against her white undergarments as he unfastened the petticoat and peeled it from her shoulders, sliding it down over her hips, so she stood in her chemise and corset. From all sides she could see them, him dark and dangerous in his evening clothes, her pale and exposed in her white undergarments.

"Should I apologize?" Her voice was throaty and inviting, even to her own ears.

Evan smiled, the slow, roguish grin that never failed to make her heart skip a beat. "Never." His hand flattened over her stomach as he plucked the string of her corset. "I reveled in every moment of it. It was quite the most . . . uplifting evening I've ever had at the theater." The corset came loose, he pressed against her, and Felicity felt the hard, heavy length of him at her back. Uplifted, indeed.

He threw the corset on the floor and then his hands covered her breasts. Her back arched and she gasped, her hands reaching backward for him, trying to anchor herself against the storm brewing inside her body. His mouth was on her neck again, kissing, sucking gently, teeth grazing her skin just hard enough to make her flinch. "Evan," she gasped.

"Dear God, I love the way you say my name." He yanked at the string of her chemise, then pulled it down to bare her breasts. Felicity let her head fall back as his hands cupped her. His touch was firm, not rough, squeezing and then feathering fingertips. He played with her nipples until

111

she squirmed, drawing a low laugh from him. His mouth opened in hot, wet kisses on her shoulders and neck, until she managed to turn her head. When his lips took hers, a charge went through her; her toes curled and her fingers flexed, digging into the fabric of his coat to hold him to her.

"Felicity." His voice rasped in her ear. "Tell me you've done this before . . ."

Head swimming, she nodded once. She could barely hear his exhalation of relief and then cool air swirled around her knees. She pried open her eyes a little and watched in the mirror as he slowly drew up the hem of her chemise. Her belly clenched in excitement, knowing what was coming, and her knees felt weak. When the chemise grazed her waist, Evan's breath hissed in her ear. "So beautiful." He kissed her again, his palm flat on her thigh, sliding up, up, up—

Felicity arched as his hand settled between her legs, warm and big. "So soft," whispered Evan, his voice guttural. His fingers stirred, and she whimpered. It had been a long time since any man had touched her there, but she was more than ready. He stroked, his fingers easing deeper between her thighs, and she almost fell off the stool at the first touch there, on the nexus of nerves. "So wet," said Evan, a taut undercurrent of need in his voice.

"Yes," she almost sobbed. "I want more—I want you— *Evan* . . ."

With a sudden movement he spun her around in his arms, his mouth claiming hers ruthlessly. Felicity surged against him, winding her arms around his neck. His hands went to her bottom, and when he lifted her, she curled her legs around his waist. Still kissing her, he turned and took a few steps before setting her down—on the worktable, she realized.

"Take this off." He flicked the drooping chemise. As she struggled out of it, he stripped off his coat and waistcoat. Felicity threw her garment aside, unabashedly baring herself to his gaze. Even though the lantern behind him was the sole source of light in the room, his eyes seemed to blaze with a light of their own.

"God almighty," he whispered.

"Take off your shirt," she said unsteadily. In white shirtsleeves, his shoulders looked incredibly broad and strong.

His wicked grin flashed again as he jerked at his cravat, almost ripping off the cloth before pulling the shirt over his head. In the low light, he was still magnificent, lean and strong. "As you command, love." He stepped forward, between her knees, clasping his hands around her hips and pulling her forward until they were pressed together from thigh to chest. For a moment they clung to each other.

Dimly Felicity wondered if he felt the same unnerving sense of oneness that she did. Even the feverish haze of desire seemed to recede for a moment as she wallowed in the strength of his arms around her, the steady thump of his heart beneath her cheek, and the feel of his breath on her shoulder. And in that moment, Felicity thought she'd never wanted anything so much, in all her life, as she wanted this to last forever.

He put one finger under her chin and tipped up her face. For a moment he just looked at her, something like wonder softening his face. Felicity stared back, helpless to look away. Why couldn't he have been a lace merchant or an attorney, she thought with some despair, someone—*anyone*—who might have contemplated forever with her?

To quell those thoughts she reached for him. She was not a fool; she knew what she was getting into.

When she put her hands behind his head and pulled him back to kiss her, his hands began to wander freely over her body. Shivers ran through her as his palms glided over her shoulders, her back, her hips. When his hands covered her breasts, she jolted upright, and he pressed her backward to lie atop her cloak.

"This table," he rasped, "is the perfect height."

It was higher than a regular table, to make it easier for the seamstresses while cutting. A wild, reckless smile crossed her face. "For what, my lord?"

He touched his finger to her lips. "Evan. Say it."

"Evan," she whispered.

His hand closed on her breast, compressing the flesh and rolling her nipple between his thumb and forefinger. Felicity arched off the table. "Again."

"Evan," she gasped. He bent over her and put his mouth where his fingers had been, suckling hard on her erect nipple. She flung her arms out, shuddering even as she pressed into his mouth.

"Again," he commanded, his fingers trailing down her stomach.

"Evan," she whimpered, her thighs tensing as he urged her legs farther apart. She gave a strangled moan as his palm moved to cover her center, now pulsing with want.

"When we are alone together, like this"—his fingers dipped into the soft, wet folds between her legs—"you are my lord and master, Felicity. You've enslaved me—you command me—"

She forced open her eyes. He loomed over her, dark and gorgeous and bare, his strong hands stroking her body into delirium, his blazing eyes fixed on her. "Make love to me, Evan," she said on a sigh. "Please."

His mouth curved before he bent his head again, to her other breast. Felicity barely had time to marvel at his words before he swept her away on a tide of sensation, with his mouth and with his hands.

Just when she felt herself approaching the brink, he pushed himself up. Leaving her gasping and tense on the table, he stepped back. "Just a moment," he said, his voice tight.

"Hurry," she moaned. Her heart was racing so hard, her pulse seemed to reverberate through her whole body.

Evan smiled, that dangerous feral smile, and turned around to fetch the lantern. He set it down beside her and pushed the shutter open all the way. "You'll drive me mad," he said as he unfastened his trousers. His eyes seemed to feast on her bare skin.

She rolled her head coyly. Her hair had come undone, and was spread across the table and her shoulders. "It would only be fair."

"Oh?" He stepped out of his shoes and trousers and kicked them aside. "How long have you wanted me?"

Her face heated. "The day you drove us to Soho Square . . ."

"My darling," he said, running his hands back up her legs, "I wanted you since the moment I laid eyes on you." Palm on her belly, his thumb dipped lower, pushing inside her for a moment, and then she felt his erection there, thick and hard. She was so wet, so ready, he slid home easily, but the fullness made her catch her breath. When he was deep inside her, Evan paused. "Try to wait for me, darling."

Her whole body was throbbing with incipient release. "I—I can't—"

115

"Try." He grasped her by the hips and pulled her toward the edge of the table until she had to hook her legs around his waist again for balance. And then he began to move, hard and steady but not nearly fast enough, flexing his spine with each thrust so that he seemed to touch something inside her that fractured Felicity's mind into pieces. She gripped his wrists, struggling to breathe, trying to hold back the approaching flood. "Evan," she begged, tears leaking down her temples. "I can't wait—"

"Yes," he rasped, and she let go. Pleasure roared through her as his thrusts grew harder, faster. The first wave had barely started to subside when he touched her. Felicity screamed at the intensity of the feeling, and Evan gave a harsh bark of laughter. "Again," he ordered, stroking her in time with the plunging of his hips against hers. Incredibly the pleasure peaked anew, until she was almost crying from it, and then Evan thrust deep and threw back his head and gave a shout of elation.

It seemed an hour before she could hear anything but her own ragged breath. When she managed to focus her gaze, she saw only Evan, leaning over her. His hands still gripped her hips, and he was still inside her. A sheen of perspiration slicked his skin, and he wore a heavy-lidded expression that put her in mind of early mornings.

He raised his head. Gently, almost reverently, he lifted her face to his. This kiss was different: soft, yearning, the sort of kiss a man in love might give. Felicity returned it with fervor, wondering if he would feel the same thing.

"Was that satisfactory?" he murmured, his lips brushing hers.

"Very." She ran her fingers through his hair.

"And it was only my first try." He pressed another tender kiss on her mouth. "Take me to bed, love."

116

Felicity's heart quivered at the last word. If only she *were* his love. She sensed she could find herself head over heels for him, with very little provocation.

But for tonight, this was enough; it would have to be. She pulled her crumpled cloak around her, took him by the hand, and led him upstairs to her bed.

Chapter Ten

The next several days were the grandest in human history, to Evan's mind.

Part of it was the anticipation of beginning the Vine Street project. He always felt a surge of energy and excitement when his plans, so long in the making, started to coalesce into stone and iron and plaster. He spent his days in the architect's office now, poring over last-minute alterations and adjustments.

It was true that Madame Follette's still sat in the middle of the street, occupied and open for business, while the last of the other tenants drove away in laden wagons, but Evan had a plan for that as well. He spoke to Mr. Jackson, who owned the Bond Street shop Felicity wanted. Jackson understood his request, but was dithering. What if Evan lost interest in the shop after a few months and declined to pay his guarantee, the man wanted to know. Evan was somewhat handicapped by not using Grantham for the negotiations, but thought he was getting on well enough without his customary solicitor. Sooner or later he and Jackson would find a way to agree, and then Felicity would have the shop her heart desired, he would have free rein in Vine Street . . . and he would have her.

Every evening, after Madame Follette's closed, he went to her. When he discovered that she had been accustomed to getting something to eat from the chophouse nearby, he began bringing dinner. They ate in her cozy sitting room, where she showed him sketches she had made for clients—who now included his mother and sister—and he recounted how he'd become enchanted with building. They talked of their childhoods, hers in a busy London shop and his in rural Wales, and discovered they almost shared a birthday, being born just three days apart in October.

By tacit agreement neither brought up the relocation. Evan had promised he would find suitable premises for her; she had said she trusted him. They talked of everything else, and then they went to bed together, where no words were necessary to build a deeper bond between them than any Evan had ever experienced.

His visits grew longer and longer, until one morning he woke with Felicity in his arms and the sun in his face. And when she opened her eyes and gave him a sleepy smile, her golden hair wild around her bare shoulders, Evan had the thought that *she* was the missing piece in his life. Ever since he'd walked into Follette's salon and laid eyes on her, he kept feeling the same sense of contentment, as if life was now complete, and finally he admitted it was because of her.

And rushing her out of Vine Street would ruin it.

Accordingly, when he returned home around dawn one morning, after a night spent making her cry out his name in rapture, to find one of Grantham's clerks drowsing on his doorstep, his first reaction was to scowl. He knew what the man had come about, and he didn't want to face it. His signature was needed to begin the demolition, and Evan had purposely not given it yet. He sent the man off with a

119

curt promise to visit Grantham's office in a few hours, but despite intense efforts while he washed, shaved, and changed, Evan had thought of no ideal solution to his problem when he was shown into the solicitor's office.

Grantham was as blunt as usual. "How do you progress with the immovable modiste?"

Evan turned his back to hide his expression. Just the thought of Felicity made him want to smile, even when Grantham called her that. "Reasonably well," he said, not directly answering the question.

"Thirty pounds per annum in the heart of Mayfair? It sounds nigh impossible to me."

"I gave her my word." He just needed Mr. Jackson to see reason. It was beginning to bother him that the man was delaying so long, and not for the first time Evan wished he could set Grantham on it.

Unfortunately he knew what Grantham would say: *Don't do it.* He would guess at once why Evan was so keen to guarantee Felicity's lease, and he would baldly ask if any woman was worth sixty pounds a year. Since Evan's answer to that query was a strong *yes,* even inching toward *worth any amount,* he had avoided the whole topic with his friend.

"You know as well as I do that your word was not a binding contract," Grantham reminded him. "Unlike these." He tapped a stack of papers, signed and stamped by the Commissioner of Woods and Fields, which had approved the Vine Street endeavor. "It's time to get on with it, Carmarthen."

"I know," Evan snapped. It was not simply his decision, now that significant money was at stake, including Treasury funds. Investors and tradesmen were waiting on him to give the order to proceed, and they didn't give a damn about Felicity's consent.

120

But he couldn't force her out before he presented her with an alternative. She was fiercely devoted to her shop, and she ran it well; it wasn't her fault that fashionable London kept moving westward, or that the development of Regent Street had cleaved her from that part of town. Madame Follette's meant as much to her as Carmarthen Castle meant to him.

There seemed no way he could press forward on schedule with Vine Street and still please Felicity; delaying the demolition would ruin his reputation, while breaking his word to Felicity . . .

Might ruin the rest of his life.

"Well. You should thank me, then," said Thomas Grantham with a cocky smile. "I have solved the problem."

Evan frowned. "What? You found premises?"

"No, I have found the means to extricate you from that devil's bargain you seem determined to keep." Grantham leaned forward and held out a sheaf of paper. "You told me to send someone to query the residents of Vine Street. Watson turned up a stray bit of gossip, which he followed on a whim, and it led him to this."

He flipped the pages. It was an affidavit, signed by a Mrs. Mary Cartwright. "What is this?"

"Mary Cartwright was a seamstress for many years at Madame Follette's. She was turned off last year when the daughter took over. It seems she's grown bitter over that, and was all too eager to tell Mr. Watson every rumor and complaint she ever had with Mrs. Dawkins."

"What has this got to do with our *problem?*" asked Evan testily. It was wrong to call Felicity a problem, even though she was at the center of the chaos in his life.

"Read it." Grantham took off his spectacles and began polishing them with a handkerchief. "I'll wait."

121

With an odd sense of foreboding, Evan sat down and read. Much of it was minor complaints, such as the time Sophie-Louise altered a gown Mrs. Cartwright had made without telling her first, or how Mrs. Cartwright's pay was withheld once over a ruined bolt of lace, but on the third page, Evan saw what had pleased his solicitor so much.

Sophie-Louise Follette had fled Paris at the height of the Terror with the family who employed her as a ladies' maid, the comte and comtesse de Challe. They were stopped at the port, where the comte and his wife were detained while Sophie-Louise was allowed to get on the ship bound for England. Apparently thinking the revolutionaries guarding the port wanted to steal their money, the comtesse de Challe gave Sophie-Louise a notable—and very valuable— set of diamonds for safekeeping and urged her to continue on to London and wait for them there. Sophie-Louise took the diamonds, made it to England, and then sold the gems as if they were her own. With the money she bought Number Twelve Vine Street and became a modiste.

Mrs. Cartwright alleged that Sophie-Louise had confessed it all to her years ago, when they were working very late one night. The Frenchwoman had sworn her to secrecy at the time. Mrs. Cartwright had kept the secret because her employment depended on it, but now that Sophie-Louise and Felicity had served her so ill, she felt no obligation to remain quiet any longer.

Evan sat like a statue. The shop was purchased with stolen jewels. Grantham knew they could use this to coerce Sophie-Louise to sell the shop, and at a far lower price than Evan had expected to pay. And if the comte de Challe, or his descendants, could be located, they could send Sophie-Louise to prison.

Felicity would be devastated. She would lose everything she loved—and she would blame him.

"Do you believe this?" Evan asked, his thoughts racing.

Grantham shrugged. "It's got a tinge of revenge, but I made a few enquiries. Mrs. Dawkins—who married Josiah Dawkins in 1795, according to the parish of St. Martin's—purchased that building in September of 1794. She paid in full, and I can find no record of a mortgage. Indeed, Mrs. Cartwight said Mrs. Dawkins was quite proud of the fact that she owned the building outright." He slid the spectacles back on his face. "Another interesting fact is that her daughter is likely not Josiah's child. There's a record of her age that suggests she was born before her mother's marriage."

It struck him like a slap to the face. Felicity was illegitimate. Her shop was built with stolen funds. Her mother was a thief and a liar.

And God help him, he wanted her anyway. He wanted her for the way her eyes lit up, for the teasing smile she gave him, for the way she blushed when he murmured seduction in her ear. He wanted to have her in his arms, in his bed, in his heart.

He folded the affidavit and slid it into his coat pocket. "Find them," he said quietly.

"Find whom?" Grantham's brows went up. "Carmarthen, this will ensure the Dawkinses cooperate, quickly and easily. Even if there's no legal recourse, one whiff of illegitimacy or thievery—from an aristocratic employer, no less—would ruin their name and trade."

"The diamonds." Evan got to his feet. "Find the de Challe diamonds, and buy them."

His solicitor stared at him as if he'd lost his mind. "Do what?"

"Buy the bloody diamonds! All of them!" He ran his hands over his head. He had no idea what he'd do with them, but it would gain him time to think of something.

"Carmarthen." Thomas Grantham rose from his chair and leaned over his desk. He lowered his voice. "What are you contemplating?"

"I don't know," he admitted, "but get those diamonds. If you can discover all this, I presume that shan't be a problem."

Grantham looked at him askance. "We don't need them to pressure Mrs. Dawkins."

"But I want them," he said through his teeth. He didn't have to explain himself to Grantham—not that he *could* explain, even to himself. "Will you find them or not?"

"Yes," said the other man after a moment. "If you wish."

Evan gave a curt nod and yanked on his coat. "Let me know when you have them. Until then, not a word of this to anyone. And learn what happened to the comte de Challe." He strode from the office, his brain roiled with uncertainty.

Chapter Eleven

Humming quietly, Felicity went down the stairs to open the salon. She ought to be tired, since Evan had spent the night again and only left two hours before Alice and Sally arrived for the day, but these days she hardly seemed to need sleep. She blushed a little at the thought of how Evan kept her awake. If she let her mind dwell on it too long, she'd end up staring into space, smiling like a fool in love.

Love. Even the word brought a bittersweet smile to her face. She had known that man was dangerous the first day she saw him, but she hadn't expected to fall so hard for him. He was an aristocrat while she was in trade, yet he treated her as his equal in intelligence and judgment. He listened to her, even when she spoke about the challenges of pleasing Lady Marjoribanks, who unfailingly requested gowns made in the least flattering colors—sometimes several within one gown. He amused her with stories of the things he'd found inside old buildings, from animal skeletons and diaries to the time his workmen tore down a wall and discovered some malicious maid, in the distant past, had emptied chamber pots into a hole in the wall. He brought dinner every night, which—after a long day that hardly allowed time to think, let alone eat—won her heart more than jewels ever could have.

To herself, Felicity admitted she was in love with him. To him . . . She didn't dare say the word. She was under no illusions that he would fall in love with her, but if she professed her love aloud, it would prompt him to point out that he never promised her love. If she kept it to herself, Felicity reasoned, she could pretend it was still possible that he might one day return the feeling.

She went through the shop and unbolted the door, opening it to let in some fresh air while she swept the steps. Vine Street was quiet these days; every other tenant had left. Felicity kept her eyes on her own steps as she whisked the broom from side to side, not wanting to think about the impending mess. Evan had given his word that he would help her relocate, and she had promised to trust him. He hadn't shown her a new shop in some time, though, and if she started thinking about it, she would wonder if he'd come to regret his promise, and if he'd end up forcing her out after all in spite of the wicked pleasures they shared in her bed every night. Therefore, Felicity tried not to think about it much. She didn't want anything to ruin the glow of happiness inside her, not yet.

A carriage turned into the deserted street as she finished sweeping. For a moment her heart skipped; could it be Evan? It was still early for clients. But it was a hackney coach, and when it stopped in front of Follette's and the door opened, a familiar figure stepped down.

Felicity's eyes rounded. "Mama!" She dropped her broom and hurried to help her mother. "What are you doing here?"

Sophie-Louise drew herself up and pinned a stern look on her. "I have come to save my shop, that's what I am doing. What do you mean by this suggestion we sell?" She pulled a letter from her reticule and flourished it in front of Felicity.

She winced. After Evan had given his word to help them relocate, she'd written to tell her mother. That had been part of *her* promise to Sophie-Louise, that she would write every fortnight about how the shop was going on. Her mother had demanded it as part of her agreement to take a holiday. "Yes, Mama. It's time to sell, but—"

Sophie-Louise flipped her hand in disgust. "Never!" She marched into the shop, leaving Felicity to show the driver where to deposit her mother's large valise. Felicity eyed that with alarm. It looked like her mother meant to stay. Not only would that put the shop into an uproar, it would end Evan's visits.

Her mother had gone straight up to the workroom, where everyone greeted her with cries of surprise. Sophie-Louise was in her element, hugging Alice and Sally, sharing a quiet exchange with Selina, whose face was flushed with delight. She wanted to see everyone's work, offering comments and compliments, until she paused in front of a gown on the wooden figure. "For which client is this?" she asked in surprise.

Felicity cleared her throat. "The Countess of Carmarthen, Mama." Evan's mother and sister had indeed come to Follette's, and ordered a good number of gowns. Unsurprisingly, the countess wanted something bold and modern, and Felicity had taken great pains to use the fashionable touches that would most flatter Lady Carmarthen. As a result it looked nothing like the gowns produced under Sophie-Louise.

Sophie-Louise's gaze narrowed, but she only said, "I see."

The day passed in a blur. Sophie-Louise resumed control of the shop as if she'd never been gone, leaving Felicity feeling oddly disgraced. She busied herself with her own work, focusing on Lady Carmarthen's gown and trying hard not to think of the lady's son. She managed to send a note to Evan around midday, informing him her mother had returned and he shouldn't call on her that night.

Her throat felt tight as she sealed it, unable to keep back the thought that it was likely the beginning of the end, if not the outright end, of their affair. She could hardly go to him, and he couldn't come to her while her mother was living with her again.

And for several days he didn't come. At first Felicity was relieved, but soon it turned to black despair. She missed him. She missed his wry smile, the timbre of his voice, the touch of his hands. She missed being able to do as she wished, without her mother's sharp eye observing everything. Every night her mother interrogated her about some facet of the business until Felicity could have screamed.

Henry came only briefly, long enough to tell his mother he was in love and planned to marry Katherine Grant. Sophie-Louise flew into ecstasy, demanding to meet the young lady and insisting on making her bride clothes, and then she utterly pardoned Henry for sending her away from the shop. Once again Henry could do no wrong, and Felicity had to defend every decision.

But the subject she most dreaded did not come up. Sophie-Louise railed against the development of Vine Street, but she didn't specifically ask about the man in charge of it. Felicity hoped that was out of ignorance, but finally her mother brought it up.

"Tell me about Carmarthen," she said one night as they sewed under the lamplight. It had been gray and grim all day, making Vine Street seem even more desolate than usual, and now the storm had arrived, thunder growling overhead and rain beating down. Felicity spared a worried thought for the leaky roof, and said a quick prayer Evan would yet locate some other suitable premises. She was sure her mother would agree to move in an instant if something like that Bond Street shop could be found.

She dragged her mind back to her mother's question. "He's bought everything else in the street. He wants to buy Follette's as well, so he can rebuild everything like it is in Regent Street."

"No, Felicity, tell me about *him*." Sophie-Louise turned a sharp gaze on her. "I hear he has been often to the shop, even in the evening."

The needle slipped right through the fabric, past her thimble, into the pad of her finger. Felicity winced. "He's an earl. His mother and sister ordered several gowns."

"He drove you out several times. Alice tells me he's very handsome."

Felicity pulled too hard on her thread, and it broke. "What are you asking, Mama?"

Her mother lifted one shoulder. "Is it Follette's he wants?"

She looked up and met her mother's eyes defiantly. "Yes."

Sophie-Louise didn't look convinced. "How will he react when he does not get Follette's?"

Felicity hesitated, then put down her sewing. "Mama, we have to sell." Sophie-Louise gathered breath to reply, and Felicity held up one hand. "He's right about Vine Street. It's falling apart, no longer fashionable or genteel. Our roof leaks. Every other building has been sold, and will be torn down any day now. Soon our clients won't be able to drive to our door, and the shop will be filled with dust."

Her mother's eyes snapped. "How can you defend this? This shop, it is my life!"

"Relocating is the only way to save it!" Felicity pleaded. "He's made a generous offer—"

"But what has he offered you?" Sophie-Louise demanded. "I will not sell to a man who trifles with my daughter, not even if he offers me ten thousand pounds." Shocked, Felicity fell back in her chair. Her mother's mouth firmed. "I have been waiting all week to hear about him. Can I not see the shadow that crosses your face every time he is mentioned? Henri tells me a little, Alice and Sally a little more, and Selina tells me the most: that you looked like a woman in love. But he has not come to call, nor have you spoken of him. If he has broken your heart, I will never forgive him, nor will I do anything to help him."

"Mama . . ." Her voice trailed off, stunned.

Sophie-Louise raised her brows. "Why do you think I came back to London? It's very pleasant in Brighton. Sea-bathing is a delight."

A full minute of silence reigned. Finally Felicity wet her lips. "He promised me nothing," she said softly. "I fell in love with him knowing it would never lead to anything. You mustn't blame him."

Her mother made a scoffing noise.

Felicity sighed. "Either way, it doesn't matter. I've not heard from him in days. Whatever was between us . . . is over."

∞

Evan walked the streets of London for what seemed like hours before he finally turned into Vine Street.

The threatening sky had given way to a full-blown storm, and he was thoroughly soaked. Despite being only ten o'clock, it felt like the middle of the night, so dark had the day been. And that suited his mood.

He stood on the pavement across from Follette's, eyes fixed on the lights in the topmost windows. He knew the rooms well, after the many nights he'd spent there, talking and laughing and making love with Felicity. Just being here again after so many days away made his heart ache. God, he missed her.

Her note, warning him that her mother had returned and he shouldn't visit, had been both a relief and a cruelty. Cruel, because he thought he'd never needed her more. Relief, because it excused him from seeing her with such turmoil in his heart and mind.

Could he let her go? Could he keep her?

Grantham thought he was deranged. His mother was shocked. Evan had felt he had to tell them what he planned to do, but neither had helped put his mind at ease. So here he was, in the pouring rain, as wretched as any schoolboy.

Shadows at the window moved. Suddenly the curtain was drawn aside, and there she was, wrestling with the window, trying to pry it open a few inches. Evan's heart gave a great leap at the sight of her, and before he knew it his feet had begun moving, taking him across the street. Hesitant no longer, he raised his hand and pounded on the door to make her hear him over the storm.

Several minutes later a light glowed in the salon. Holding the lamp aloft, Felicity came forward and peered out into the darkness. Her face blanked in astonishment when she saw him, and she hurried forward to slide back the bolt and open the door.

"I know it's late," he said before she could speak. "I had to see you. May I come in?"

Regret flashed over her face. "Evan—"

"Please, darling," he said. "Hear me out."

At the endearment, something lit in her eyes, and a tiny smile curved her lips. With a nod, she stepped back and let him in, closing the door against the rain behind him.

"Who is there? Is it Henri?" Another woman came into the salon, lamp in hand.

Evan knew at once it was Felicity's mother. Sophie-Louise was the same height as her daughter, a little plumper and a lot grayer. The same blue eyes snapped in her face as she swept an imperious glance over him. "What is the meaning of this, sir?"

"Mama, this is Lord Carmarthen," said Felicity. "My mother, Mrs. Dawkins, sir."

"A great pleasure to make your acquaintance, Mrs. Dawkins." He bowed very formally, ignoring the rain that dripped off his shoulders.

"My lord." Mrs. Dawkins dipped a shallow curtsy. "The shop is closed."

"I know. I apologize for disturbing you, but . . ." His gaze slid back to Felicity, who wore an expression of composed anxiety. "I had to speak to Miss Dawkins and could not wait even until tomorrow."

"Ah. What have you come to say?"

"Mama," said Felicity under her breath.

132

Evan turned back to the older woman. "Mrs. Dawkins, I would like to purchase this building. My solicitor, Mr. Grantham, has written to you several times about it."

She sniffed. "I recall his letters."

"In your absence, I approached your daughter, Miss Dawkins." Again he looked at her. What would she say to this? "She repeated, very firmly, your opposition to selling, but at last we struck a bargain: She would encourage you to sell to me if, and when, a suitable location was found elsewhere for Madame Follette's."

Mrs. Dawkins looked at her daughter with furious dismay. Felicity flushed, but gave a small nod.

Evan plowed onward. "We located a fine shop in Bond Street, but the rent asked was too high. Believing that Miss Dawkins found it perfectly suited to her needs, I negotiated with the landlord. I have come tonight to offer you the premises at Bond Street and Clifford Street for the rent of thirty pounds per annum."

Felicity gasped. "How on earth—?"

He'd bought the whole damn building from Mr. Jackson, just concluded that afternoon. He'd explain that later. "In addition, I am increasing my offer for this building by two hundred pounds," Evan said, holding up one hand to stay her. "Can we agree, Mrs. Dawkins?"

The older woman's face grew stern. "Am I to agree to this now? I have not seen this shop, and even then, we could not possibly remove from these quarters before Michaelmas."

"Mrs. Dawkins, workmen will begin demolishing Vine Street within the week. All the papers are signed and filed. It is imperative that you relocate at the soonest possible opportunity."

Her eyes flashed. She set down her lamp on the counter and crossed her arms. "My answer is the same I gave to your presumptuous lawyer: no."

"Mama, the shop he mentions is perfect," said Felicity urgently. "A vast step up for Follette's."

Her mother shot her a sharp look, but Evan thought there was a crack in her adamant refusal. He plunged his hand into one pocket as he crossed the room toward her. "Perhaps this will alter your decision." He pulled out a diamond bracelet and laid it on the counter, where it glittered in the lamplight.

Felicity, who had followed him, choked. "Goodness!"

Evan kept his eyes on Mrs. Dawkins. She frowned at the bracelet. He pulled out a necklace and put it next to the bracelet. Mrs. Dawkins's eyes flared in recognition, but she said nothing. He added a pair of earrings and a brooch before she spoke. "The diadem," was all she said, in a flat voice.

"Broken up," he told her. That was the only piece Grantham had failed to buy, because it had been split up several years ago.

Felicity held her lamp higher over the jewels, her face pale. "What is this?"

"It is a threat." Mrs. Dawkins looked at Evan grimly. "Sell, or you will expose me."

"No." He gazed back evenly, but reached for Felicity's hand. "It's not a threat." He glanced at Felicity, and smiled to banish her anxious expression. "I hope it will be a wedding gift."

Her lips parted, and her beautiful eyes grew bright. Evan folded her hand between his. "I've been lost without you these last few days. I love you, darling. Marry me, I beg you."

134

She looked stunned, raising a trembling hand to touch his cheek. "You love me?"

"Madly," he confessed. "Didn't you guess?"

An incredulous smile spread across her face. "I was so afraid to hope you might . . ."

His grip tightened on her hands. "Then . . . ?"

"Yes," she said, beginning to laugh. "Yes!"

"And?" he prompted, now grinning like a fool himself.

Her smile grew warm, and she put her arms around his neck, in spite of his dripping wet coat. "I love you, Evan."

He had time to brush his lips across hers before Sophie-Louise Dawkins cleared her throat. Felicity's mother was still pale, her eyes fixed on the diamond parure on the counter. "Where did you get these?"

"Here and there," said Evan vaguely. "All entirely legal, of course. The comte de Challe never made it out of France. It's been more than twenty years since his jewels went missing, which means no one can be prosecuted." He pictured Felicity sprawled in his bed, wearing the diamonds and nothing else. "And now they're mine, to give as I wish."

Felicity, looking between them, shook her head in confusion. "What are you talking about?"

Her mother reached out and gingerly touched the pendant stone in the necklace, a stunning diamond the size of an acorn. "These were the property of the comtesse de Challe," she said in a low voice. "My mistress in France. When the Terror came, she wished to flee. The comte delayed, to gather funds and valuables, and by the time we set off for England, the revolutionaries were at our heels. We were detained in Calais. My master thought they would be robbed of everything, so he gave me the jewels and some money and instructed me to continue to England and

135

wait for them there." She raised haunted eyes to them. "I waited for months, monsieur. Months with no word, no aid. The money was gone and I—" Her gaze veered to Felicity, then away. "I had to support myself."

Evan guessed what she left unsaid: She'd been expecting a child, without a husband. His arms tightened around Felicity. Those diamonds had given her a safe home, a happy childhood, and then a livelihood. Thank heavens Sophie-Louise had sold them. "I don't blame you," he said quietly.

"You bought this shop with money from these," whispered Felicity numbly. "Oh, Mama . . ."

Mrs. Dawkins drew a deep breath. "Monsieur le comte, I accept your offer. If you are to be my son-in-law, I will not fear you sending me to prison. You may buy this shop, because . . ." She smiled, a bit uncertainly, at Felicity. "I trust my daughter's judgment. If she says the other premises are perfect, that is all I need to know. She has taken excellent care of Follette's in my absence."

"Thank you, Mama," said Felicity softly.

Her mother raised an eyebrow, glancing from the diamonds to Evan and back to her daughter. "I believe I should be thanking you," she said gently, and turned toward the stairs. "I am going now. You may kiss him to your heart's content." She left, taking one lamp with her.

Evan reached for the necklace. "How soon do you want to be married?"

Felicity pressed one hand to her forehead, looking overwhelmed. "I have commissions to finish—your mother—"

"She can wait. I cannot." He fastened the necklace around her neck and admired it, lying just above the swells of her bosom. "Next week?"

She gasped. "I haven't a gown!"

"Wear the blue one that you wore to Grantham's office. I nearly lost my wits when you walked in." He eyed the diamonds again. "And wear these."

She touched them. "How did you know about these? And why did you buy them?"

"I bought them so no one could ever harass your mother about them," he said, ignoring the first question. He'd explain about that later. "So we're agreed: The wedding will be next week."

Felicity began to laugh. "Must you win every negotiation between us?" He put his hands on her hips and boosted her to sit on the counter, putting his face level with her bosom. At the first touch of his lips on her skin, her laughter faded. "Yes," she breathed, "next week would suit me perfectly."

Evan grinned, and blew out the lamp. "Excellent. Now kiss me, to your heart's content."

In the darkness she smiled, pulling him close. "That will take the rest of my life."

If you enjoyed *A Fashionable Affair*, please consider leaving a review online to help other readers. Thank you!

Dressed to Kiss

This novella was conceived as part of a collection featuring the dressmakers (and bookkeeper) of Madame Follette's shop. If you're curious to know how Selina caught the Duke of Barrowmore . . . or how Delyth fared with her very fashionable clients, the Merrithews . . . and how Felicity's brother Henry fell for Miss Katherine Grant, don't miss *Dressed to Kiss,* an anthology with stories from Madeline Hunter, Megan Frampton, and Myretta Robens.

Caroline Linden was born a reader, not a writer. She earned a math degree from Harvard University and wrote computer software before turning to fiction. Since then, her books have won the NEC-RWA Reader's Choice Award, the Daphne du Maurier Award, the NJRW Golden Leaf Award, and RWA's RITA Award, and have been translated into seventeen languages around the world. Visit her at www.CarolineLinden.com or find her on Facebook (AuthorCarolineLinden) and Twitter (@Caro_Linden).

Visit www.carolinelinden.com/signup.html to join her VIP readers' group and get notified of all her new book releases, get sneak peeks at work-in-progress, and a free short story exclusively for members.

Printed in the USA
CPSIA information can be obtained
at www.ICGtesting.com
LVHW011013180823
755627LV00017B/208

9 780997 149432